SOUL, SUN & STARS

A SIRIANS SERIES NOVELLA

K.M. DAVIDSON

✶

Copyright © 2025 by K.M. Davidson

All rights reserved.

No part of this publication may be reproduced, stored, or transmitted in any form or by any means, electronic, mechanical, photocopying, recording, scanning, or otherwise—except in the case of brief quotations embodied in critical articles or reviews—without written permission from its publisher.

The author expressly prohibits using this book in any matter to train artificial intelligence (AI) technologies for the purpose of generating text, including works in the same genre or style as this book.

This novel is entirely a work of fiction. The names, characters, and incidents portrayed in it are the work of the author's imagination. Any resemblance to actual persons, living or dead, events or localities is entirely coincidental and not intended by the author.

K.M. Davidson asserts the moral right to be identified as the author of this work.

Interior Map Design by Brian Andersen
Edited by Wonder and Wander Editing Co.
Cover Design by K.M. Davidson
Remy & Reva Art by Rami fon Verg (@ramifonverg)

N
W
E
S
The Scorpio Palace
The Scorpion Lake
The Black Lake
The Black Avalanche
The Red Raven
Ghita
Cerelia
The Forbidden Island
Gylly Tower
The Clips
Main Town
Eldamain
Orion's Lake
The Great Karasi
Vega
Saros
Castle of Andromeda
The Red River
Rian
The Rocky Points
Teslin
Saros Tower
Sato
The Ravens Wood
Heartlake
Elvi
Mariande
Lolis
The Southern Beaches
Etherea
Chimbridge
Eryphos
Rigel's Keep
The Sand Dunes & Beaches
Blood Lake

MAGICS & THE HOUSES

HOUSE OF ECHIDNA

Founded by Sybil
Serpent and Dragon Shifters

HOUSE OF NEMEA

Founded by Garuda
Feline and Bird Shifters

HOUSE OF ARGO

Founded by Brigid
Marine Shifters

DEITIES & THE GODS

DEITIES

KUK
The Darkness, the Abyss, Dark beings

KHONSA
Choice, Magics, the Light

GODS (CHILDREN OF KUK & KHONSA)

DOLA
Goddess of Destiny & Fate

MORANA
Goddess of Death & Magic

DANICA
Goddess of Nature & the Energy of All Things, The Morning/Evening Star

ROD
God of Family, Birth, & Humanity

DEMI-GODS

CHILDREN OF MORANA

SYBIL
Magic, Founded House of Echidna

CHILDREN OF DANICA

PHOEBE
Sirian – Gravitational Energy Manipulation

TARANIS
Sirian – Lightning Manipulation

ASTERIA
Sirian – Heightened Energy Manipulation, Stars & Galaxy

DIONNE
Sirian – Heat Manipulation Variation

CHILDREN OF ROD

BRIGID
Magic, Founded House of Argo

BODHI
Immortal Human

ENKI
Immortal Human, The First King

GARUDA
Magic, House of Nemea

Author Note

This novel starts 40 years before the events in The Sirians Series. "A.V." dictates the events of this universe after the Etherean War, and it stands for ANNO VICISSITUDO. In this world it means ""IN THE YEAR OF CHANGE".

While this story is classified as "Rivals-to-Lovers", I want to warn you that by industry standards, this is **not an HEA** ("happily ever after") for the romance plot.

This love story is considered a **romantic tragedy**, so I apologize for that.

And while the ending may hurt you, I can promise you it is still wholesome.

Content Warning

This adult fantasy novel contains mature themes and content that may not be suitable for all readers. Readers are advised that the story contains depictions of violence, graphic imagery, explicit language, and scenes of a sexual nature, including Male/Male and Male/Male/Female. Additionally, the narrative explores challenging subject matters, including but not limited to death, betrayal, and psychological distress. Please exercise discretion and know that the content may trigger or be unsettling for some audiences.

This story is for those who have wandered through the shadows of loss and emerged stronger.

For the dreamers, the seekers, and the brokenhearted who found the courage to rebuild.

No matter how many times you lose your way, may you always find your way back.

*"Never forget thy fall,
O Icarus of the fearless flight,
For the greatest tragedy of them all,
Is never to feel the burning light."*

Quote attributed to Oscar Wilde

Chapter 1

Springtide 1782 A.V.

Growing up, the Black Avalanches were never anything special to me. Sure, they loomed on the horizon as menacing as ever, but I was so accustomed to their presence I never considered what lay within or beyond them.

So, when my father came to me roughly a week after my wings sprung painfully from my back following the events of drunken debauchery and told me I would be apprenticing with Voss for the remainder of my young adulthood in the Black Avalanches…

You could say I was more than a little perturbed.

"What do you mean in the Black Avalanches?" I asked, sitting upright in my bed. "You can't actually mean—"

"Voss has always found solace near the Black Avalanches," Father sighed, twirling the corners of his mustache. "He prefers solitude over community. I guess it allows him the privacy or security he's looking for."

"And he wants me to be his apprentice?" I balked, curling my lip. "I've never met the guy, despite him being your so-called friend, and you want to send me off to him?"

"Remiel," Father sighed again, heavier this time, as he ran a hand through his almost-black hair. Despite being nearly thirty years my senior, it was always fascinating how he looked barely into his thirties. "You are the first of our family to inherit the wings in generations. I don't even recall the last time I saw any Magic from the House of Echidna manifest them."

"Shouldn't that be concerning in some way?" I pursed my lips, throwing myself back down on the bed. I glared at Father from the corners of my eyes as I interlocked my hands behind my head. "It didn't feel great, I can tell you that."

In fact, it'd felt like someone took a blade to my back and carved them from my skin and bones.

Father seethed, clenching and unclenching his fist. "It is concerning, Remiel. You're eighteen and act like a child, and you have been gifted a rare trait of our House, yet you prance around like a mortal as if it were just another trick up your sleeve to whip out at the pub."

"That's not all I'm whipping out at the pub," I grumbled under my breath, and unfortunately, the old man heard me. He reached for the nearest item he could find in my room, which happened to be my winter cap, and launched it at me with a force I was not expecting.

"Voss will not tolerate immaturity, Remiel." Father stepped further into the room, pointing an accusatory finger at me. "To be accepted into his apprenticeship is a blessing from Morana. He is one of few known Magics to have an increased development of his abilities, aside from his wings. He is your only hope at mastering them and navigating any other abilities you may have."

I decided at that moment it was in my best interest if I kept my mouth shut unless I wanted the collection of crystals on my dresser to be the next thing he threw at me. His shoulders relaxed when he realized I was pretending to be complicit.

"I don't know why you've inherited the wings," Father explained, exasperated. If only he knew how I felt when they unfurled from my back in the middle of Ghita's square. "And we can't be sure if you've inherited prophesying, compulsion, or—Gods forbid—poisoned canines. Outside of the Great Karasi, Voss is your best bet at learning and honing what you did inherit. It can be an advantage as a Magic, and it could help you win favor with different kingdoms."

"Alright, Father," I agreed, if only so he'd leave my room. I rubbed a hand down the side of my face and scratched at my bare chin. "So, I leave when? And how long am I to be his apprentice?"

"Voss will decide how long your apprenticeship will last." Father took two steps out of the door before bracing himself on the frame and throwing his head over his shoulder. "And you leave tomorrow."

He walked out and down the hall without another word.

I pressed my lips into a thin line, my eye twitching as I stared up at the wooden slats of my ceiling for another moment longer, forcing a slow exhale through my pursed lips.

Deep down, I knew my father was right. I'd never met any Magics who had abilities beyond the strength, stamina, speed, and fantastical blood that came with being Other. Sure, plenty of Magics had strange eye and hair colors, small defining characteristics like snake eyes, scales, sharpened canines, or even the occasional retractable claws…

But something like wings from the House of Echidna or Nemea, or the House of Argo with their ability to manifest gills? Those were rare. Myth said when the Gods left our world, they took any hint of our shifting abilities with them.

I grunted as I heaved myself out of bed, running a hand through my disheveled hair as I stood. The memories of last night's sinful events reminded me that my father was also insinuating I should use this time with Voss to make something of myself.

I had minimal interest in having some grand purpose in this

world. Granted, that was before I knew about the wings and the possibility of other gifts, but even with that knowledge, I still had no interest.

I was content living my life like any other Magic in Ghita, Rian, or Main Town, working the pubs or shops until my dying day—whenever that would come.

A soft knock on the wall had me glowering at my open door, but it slipped from my face the moment my eyes locked with Cara's identical purple ones.

"Hey, kid," I greeted, patting the space next to me on the mattress. "Want to join me in my misery?"

She squinted at me with the look of a teenager far wiser than she should've been. "You act like Father is shipping you off to Etherea."

"We don't know this Voss," I scoffed as I reclined back on my two hands. "Mother and Father say they've known him for decades and that he's an old friend of the family, but we've never met the guy. For all we know, he could work for that country."

"Highly unlikely," Cara laughed, finally joining me on the bed. She plopped down beside me with her legs folded beneath her. "When do you leave?"

"Don't act coy, Cee." My eyes narrowed as I side-eyed her. "I know you were eavesdropping from your room, but it's tomorrow."

"I just wanted to hear the melancholy in your voice." She smirked, a canine glinting in the light. She flipped her wavy, dark brown hair over her shoulder. "I needed to confirm it was because you're leaving me."

I snickered and wrapped a curled arm over her shoulders and around her neck. I leaned all my weight onto my sister, eliciting a disgruntled growl as she tried and failed to escape my clutches.

"Why couldn't you be the one to grow wings?" I grumbled in

her ear, using my free hand to rub the top of her head. She swatted at me, curling her lip and trying again to wiggle free. I hooked my arm tighter. "It'd be far more sensible of the Gods to grant you this lovely gift."

"You just reached adulthood, Remy." Cara slipped from underneath my arm. With her weight now missing, I nearly pitched forward off the bed. She clasped her hands behind her back, rocking back and forth on her feet. "I still have four more years to manifest extra abilities."

I rolled my eyes, but my chest fluttered at the thought of my sister and me with extra gifts. If anything, so I wouldn't be alone. She already had my matching purple eyes and sharp canines, but that never meant much when, personality-wise, we were so far removed from each other.

"You better manifest wings." My head brushed the ceiling when I stood from the bed to my full height, towering over Cara. She craned her neck to look up into my eyes, which only narrowed as I stepped closer. I wagged my finger in her face. "I'll come for you on your eighteenth birthday, and we'll have words if you don't have them."

I tapped her on the tip of her button nose, and she snarled, "I'll come for *you* on my eighteenth birthday if I don't have wings and rip them off your back—"

"Gods, you're murderous." I slipped around her, calling out as I snaked around the edge of my door frame. "And I love it."

⁎⁺☾⁎⁺

I helped my mother prepare for dinner for the first time in what felt like ages.

Probably because by this time most evenings, I was already on my way to the main square in Ghita.

I watched her out of the corner of my eye as I sliced the warm bread, her concentration entirely absorbed in checking the consistency of the stew. She twirled the wooden spoon in one hand, her other flat against her lower back as her brows furrowed over her glistening purple eyes.

She'd been fighting tears since the moment I offered a hand in the kitchen.

Like my father, Mother barely looked as if age issued a number, appearing younger than she should. Where my father had the dark brown, wavy locks that Cara and I inherited, Mother's platinum white hair hung down her back in straight strands. Every other trait we got from her though, from the fair skin and slightly buttoned noses to the piercing, purple eyes.

"Momma," I softly chided, gently wrapping my hand over hers on the spoon. "Do you want me to take over? You can relax if you want."

She dragged her attention away from the big pot, locking her gaze onto me, blinking rapidly.

"Oh, Momma," I sighed, using my grip on her hand to pull her into a side hug. Her delicate hands slid around my midsection and interlocked on the other side. She pressed her cheek against my chest, burrowing into me.

"I know your father wants to help you," she explained, her Northern Pizi accent only somewhat faded after decades on the Main Continent. "But you are my baby. You have never left home before. I fear you going far."

"Not that I'm particularly thrilled about leaving either." I buried my nose on the top of her head, mumbling, "A cave in the mountains sounds pretty secure, not to mention an old Magic by my side."

"A mother has her worries." She dug a bony finger into my rib, and I squirmed away from her, but not before I caught the smile gracing her pointed features. "Don't tell your sister I said that either."

"About me being your favorite?" I called out over my shoulder just as Cara walked into the kitchen. She stopped dead in her tracks, her hands limp at her sides. Her face morphed into a sneer, but she couldn't hide the playful glint in her eyes.

"Mother," Cara chastised, resuming her graceful swagger, practically floating to the table, "don't lie to him on his final night of freedom. It's unkind."

"Who says that old man will be able to keep me tamed?" I joined Cara at the table, sinking into the wooden chair across from her. I slid the bread to the middle of the table, tucked my hands under my arms, and leaned my elbows on the chipped surface. "I've got wings now. You know I'll find the nearest form of debauchery and sneak out—"

"Remiel," Father's voice boomed from the entryway, his ominous form a silhouette in my peripheral.

I slowly rolled my eyes to the back of my head, begrudgingly twisting toward him with a pained grin. "Yes, Father dearest?" I said over Cara's barely-contained snickers.

As he stepped into the light of the house, he couldn't hide the small twitch of his lips beneath his mustache, no matter how hard he screwed his face into a scowl. "For your own benefit, I will warn you only once more that Voss has far less tolerance for *debauchery* than your mother and I do. He will know when you come and go, and he will punish you for doing so under the shroud of darkness."

I opened my mouth to retort, maybe question just how he'd punish me, but Father leveled an imposing finger at me in warning.

Considering Mother was making her way over with a wooden spoon and pot of stew in hand, it was for the best that he cut me off when he did.

"Now," Father grunted, falling heavily into the seat at the head of the table, "let's try and have a normal family meal together before Remiel goes off to start this apprenticeship with Voss. Who knows when he will let you come home for a visit."

"Normal like the mortals?" I asked, meeting Cara's hesitant gaze across the table as she leaned back in the chair with her arms crossed over her chest. "Or Remy normal?"

Father simply huffed with the ghost of a smile that mirrored our mother's.

Dinner continued just as Father requested. He and Mother shared stories about how they knew Voss, how deep his ties to our family were through our grandparents, and what exactly he said to my parents when they asked him to take me under his wing as his apprentice.

Voss simply replied, *Send him.* When I asked if that meant yes or no, Father just glared at me from the head of the table and told me not to ask that question to Voss's face.

Apparently, the man was about one-hundred-and-fifty years old, which was well into the senior end for most Magics. While our enhanced blood and abilities allowed us to live extended lifespans, we averaged roughly one-hundred-and-twenty years. There were few people who were as old as Voss. In fact, he was the youngest of the oldest Magics I'd ever heard of, all who inherited a power the world rarely ever saw from Magics anymore.

The Great Karasi was the oldest. Her age was unknown, but many said she surpassed five-hundred years old. Not only did she have prophetic powers, but it was rumored she had a sort of necromancy ability by way of creating unique potions.

The next oldest I'd heard of was some man from the House of Argo who spoke the *water language*. I had no idea what that entailed, but according to my mother who was from that House, she said it meant what it sounded like. Water spoke to him.

Leaving Cara to help Mother and Father clean up, sneaking onto our front porch, I hopped down the few wooden steps and padded into the grass with my hands in my pockets. The Black Avalanches loomed in the distance, their peaks reaching into the Heavens.

"Why would you be out here staring at the mountains you're about to spend Gods-know how long inside?" Cara said from behind me, her voice carrying with the subtle breeze.

I threw my head over my shoulder, meeting her gaze. "The view won't be the same."

She huffed a breathy chuckle, picking up her black dress as she followed me to the tree on our plot. I plopped onto the ground, waiting as she side-stepped some stray tree roots jutting from the ground. She delicately maneuvered the skirts around to sit beside me, her knee brushing mine.

"Nothing will be the same," she sighed, staring off toward the mountains looming in the skyline, the setting sun striking an ethereal glow behind them.

I leaned my head into her, and she tipped hers until our heads touched. We sat in silence for a moment, where birds chirping above our heads and our parents' soft conversation floating from the open window of our home were the only sounds around us.

"I don't know how to go about my days without you," Cara softly admitted, clasping her hand on top of mine in the grass. "You're leaving me with Mother and Father, and I'll have to suffer their schooling alone."

"You have your friends in town." I lifted away from her,

angling so I sat cross-legged beside her. "You've got the girls, and isn't there a certain male you've been—"

"Remy!" she snapped, her face breaking out into a blush. "I refuse to talk with you about romantics. Not that you know anything."

"I beg to differ!" I snorted, shoving her shoulder. "I am such a romantic. I charm one and all, so I would say that makes me more of a romantic than you."

She rolled her eyes and shook her head as she turned to stare at the mountains again.

"Besides," I smirked, reclining back on my hands, "your fellow is probably the only male in this town within our age range who I have yet to *romanticize*—"

Cara squealed, but it trailed off into a sly chortle as she lunged for me, tackling me to the ground. My own laughter followed hers, utter glee bouncing between us.

We laid outside together under the clear night sky for a while, talking about the stars and what it must feel like to fly amongst them. The true gravity of my situation would weigh on me whenever we lapsed into our comfortable silence, a sharp thorn burrowing itself deeper into the cavity beside my heart.

I had spent the majority of my life with Cara. The day she was born, I was determined to be the best big brother. I wanted to protect her and take her under my wing—only metaphorical at the time. Our parents schooled both of us in standard subjects, and in potions, although she took to the potion studying better than I ever did.

Ever since I turned sixteen, I spent most evenings and nights at the pubs in town with some other Magics, but every other moment of my free time was spent with Cara or helping Father when he'd get an influx of requests for potions, salves, and other apothecary needs.

I got the impression where I was going tomorrow was not a place of glee, at least by my normal standards.

But even more so because Cara would not be there.

I never felt alone so long as she was there, and the darkness of my mind stayed away between her joyous laughter and the sub-par ale from the pubs.

The thought of having neither brought a tightness in my chest I always tried to ignore.

Chapter 2

Father said it would take me nearly an entire day by horse to reach the base of the Black Avalanches. In an effort to avoid emotional goodbyes, I set out before dawn toward my new adventure, leaving a rose quartz behind on the table for my mother and sister.

The journey from Ghita to the mountains was as I anticipated: barren, grassy plains that made it difficult to stay awake on the trek. With less than a handful of stops to water and feed myself and the horse, it still took me until sunset before I arrived along the coast of the Black Lake, where the base of the mountains created a sloped path into their depths.

I just started wondering to myself how I would possibly call Voss down from his perch when a blur of brown and beige fell to the ground before me. The horse startled, pitching me out of the saddle, and I landed flat on my back. The wind whooshed out of me, and I wheezed awkwardly as I listened to the horse's hooves pound off into the distance.

"If this introduction is any indication of how your time with me will be," said a deep, heavily accented voice. "Then this will be my greatest challenge yet."

A deep brown hand was extended in front of me in offering. I grunted another breath of air before accepting the hand, barely putting any of my own weight into it as I rose from the ground.

"Well, we didn't anticipate a man falling from the sky," I managed to squeeze out as I rubbed my lower back, willing the breaths into my chest. "How was I supposed to be prepared for something like that?"

"You are Magic, first and foremost." He said as I brushed a combination of sand and dried grass from my body and adjusted my tunic. "You have enhanced abilities, do you not? As a Magic with a rare capability from the House of Echidna, you should have far more impressive senses."

"What the hell is that—" I finally locked eyes with the man who I had already assumed to be Voss, startling slightly.

My encounter with most elderly Magics was what one might anticipate: wrinkled, graying, hunched, smelly. For a man who was supposedly over one hundred and fifty years old, he didn't look much older than my parents.

He was a few inches shorter than me but still well over six feet tall. Where my hair hung in dark brown curls, his was stark white and spun into dreads past his shoulders, striking against his deep brown skin. He had a spattering of black stubble across his upper lip and at the edges of his chin, and dark gray eyes scrutinized me just as much as I studied him.

The man was also far more built than I was, but I had always been long and lanky in stature with barely an ounce of noticeable muscle on me. Instead, his bulged beneath a brown leather jacket that looked like it was made in Riddling, but his accent placed him from Teslin.

What separated us even further were the wings, towering behind him like a protective barrier, light beige and *feathered*, whereas mine looked as though someone stretched oiled, black leather over a skeleton.

A low rumble snapped me back to attention. "Have I met your

expectations, young *drakon?*" Voss asked, raising a bushy black eyebrow.

"Not in the slightest." I paused, pressing my lips together. I titled my head to the side. "What did you just call me?"

"*Drakon,*" Voss repeated, flicking his thumb toward the mountain as he began to walk toward the sloping pathway. I watched in delight as both wings twitched imperceptibly before collapsing like someone had crushed them, then vanishing entirely.

"What does that mean?" I asked, picking up my pace. "Also, my horse had my belongings on it. Are we going to be able to find it?"

"Your horse will not venture far," Voss chuckled, waving a hand aimlessly behind us. "After a long day of travel, it will undoubtedly stick to the lake. We will fetch your things quite easily."

I glanced over my shoulder momentarily, trying to squint toward the lake, but dusk had already started swallowing the pink-streaked sky. I turned my attention back toward the path ahead of me, dimming by the minute.

"As for the name," Voss continued, sidestepping a boulder. "It is the old Etherean language. It was what they used to call one of the scaled creatures your House could shift into."

"*One* of the *scaled* creatures?" I curled my lip. "I've never heard of it before."

"There are not many Magics that learn our heritage and the name of the creatures we all originated from." Voss shrugged, turning his head to me. "You will learn, though, and maybe you will teach generations after me."

"*Generations?*" My voice cracked. I cleared it before continuing, "Just because I have wings, you think I'm going to live for generations?"

Voss chuckled, but tension gathered in his shoulders.

If I was irritating him already, this apprenticeship would indeed be his greatest challenge.

"Whether you live an extended lifetime or not, what you are able to learn from me will benefit those who come under you as you take on your own apprentices." Voss threw his shoulders back like he proudly wore the weight he placed upon himself. "I don't accept payment to mentor. All I ask is that you find Magics with hidden abilities like yourselves. Teach them how to use those powers to their advantage, and show them not to fear their safety among mortals."

Voss stopped abruptly, twisting on his heel to look me dead in the eye. The grinding of rock echoed off the jagged walls around us.

"Strange, don't you think?" There was a predatorial glint in his glowing gray eyes as he sneered, a sharp canine peeking out. "Beings who are faster, stronger, and more than mortals, and yet *we* fear *them*."

"You've got a vendetta, don't you?" I chuckled, trying to brush off the chill that crawled up my neck.

Voss narrowed his eyes, inspecting me in silence. I shifted on my feet, my skin prickling at the scrutiny.

After what felt like a lifetime, he huffed and continued our journey into the dark mountain.

I stayed close behind him as we weaved through gaps between thick spires and jutting peaks, unable to see beyond my hand, so how he was able to navigate was beyond me. Outside of the gravel crunching beneath our feet or rocks tumbling down the slope behind us, it was eerily silent through this part of the mountain. I wasn't sure if Voss's inhabitance had scared any creatures away, but my skin crawled in the heavy darkness.

It didn't take much longer before a glowing sconce anchored

to a massive wall of rock reaching into the sky revealed an arched, wooden door. It looked like Voss had just found some random, simple wooden door and slapped some hinges on. The bronze handle was rusted and worn, as if it'd been there for ages.

"You step over this threshold," Voss began, his voice stern, "and that is your contract to follow and obey my rules. This is my home, and I expect you to treat it with respect. You will find that I have much to teach you, and you could be incredible."

I eyed him suspiciously, hoping he didn't expect his words to move me toward a greater purpose. After a single nod from me to confirm my compliance, he turned the handle and swung the door open.

Voss's cave wasn't just a rocky hole in the mountain. The walls were all supported by wooden beams that extended far up the mountain, adorned with various art pieces, strange masks, animal bones, and tapestries. The rock walls to my left and right curved, leading to what I assumed were extra halls and rooms.

Directly before me in the center of the main living area was a small brick firepit with curls of smoke wafting dozens of feet up into a perfect hole in the stone ceiling, escaping out what was presumably the only other exit than the front door.

Not that it looked like anyone with wings would be fitting through that hole.

Pushed up against the left side of the room was a decrepit couch, held together by this point with multicolored and patterned patches. On the opposite side were two simple leather chairs in mint condition. Rugs of various designs and sizes were spread across the floor haphazardly, covering most of the smooth ground.

"Your room will be the first door on the left down that hallway." Voss extended his arm out toward the dip in the wall to our right. No sooner had Voss finished his words when another figure slowly walked into view from around the opposite corner. "Just in time. This is my other apprentice, Ibis."

"Your other..." The words fell silent on my lips as I observed him, and Gods, if he didn't radiate like the sun.

Hot. Intimidating. Demanding.

His rich, brown hair curled in tight ringlets around his head, a stray strand dangling in front of his forehead, longing to be tucked back. His caramel skin even brought out natural highlights, which blended with whiskey eyes. His strong, chiseled jaw came to the point of a dimpled chin coated in a short hint of stubble. A single golden hoop hung from his earlobe, matching the one strung through his nose. A pair of loose, cotton trousers clung to every dip and curve of his body like second skin, a simple leather vest leaving his sculpted, golden chest open to the glow of the sconces on the wall.

"Ibis," the man repeated, jutting his hand between us. I raised an eyebrow at it, slowly dragging my gaze up his veiny forearms and bicep and across his broad chest, dusted with brown hair.

By the time I finally met his liquid eyes, his lip curled in a sneer, exposing a sharpened canine glinting white.

White like the large, feathered wings hanging on his back.

"You collect the ones with wings, huh?" I called to Voss from the side of my mouth, not breaking eye contact.

Even as Ibis's face hardened.

And I flicked my tongue over my own sharpened canine.

"Speaking of which," Voss interrupted, cutting through the thickening tension with his sharp voice. "Where are yours, Remiel?"

I peered over my shoulder where my wings were hidden within whatever strange place they seemed to go when I didn't want them around.

Or, more so, when they didn't want to come out.

"I don't show and tell," I smirked, locking eyes with the radiant man before me. I winked. "Unless you ask."

"Consider this us asking," Ibis spoke, his deep voice rumbling through me, his accent from Riddling. The glare he leveled me with went straight to my cock.

I straightened, rolled my neck, and closed my eyes, praying to Morana that these damned things unfurled. To add a little flare to my demonstration, I spread my arms wide, hands splayed.

A sharp tingle shot up my spine, breaking into two branches at my shoulders. The muscles pinched, and the skin felt like it was being sliced open before the wings shot out from their place, the sound like shaking out a blanket.

Not the most pleasant feeling, but the relief I always felt when they were free kept me from instinctively hunching my shoulders.

Something foreign flashed across Ibis's face fleetingly, gone before I could register what it meant.

"That looked like it may have hurt," Voss observed condescendingly, taking a few steps to stand beside Ibis with his hands clasped behind his back. His dark, silver eyes bore into me. "We'll work on that. I don't expect you to have them mastered in the slightest, considering you were just gifted them within the last month."

"Gifted." I nodded, pressing my brows together. "I wouldn't go that far. More like burdened."

Ibis audibly scoffed before turning his back on me. I startled, pursing my lips together, my gaze bouncing between Ibis's back and Voss's raised eyebrows.

"You think your wings a burden?" Voss tilted his head in that assessing yet preying manner.

I kept my gaze locked onto Ibis's silky feathers until he

disappeared down the opposite corridor from where Voss indicated my room would be.

"I want to be honest here." I pinched the bridge of my nose, shaking the image of Ibis's strong, toned figure out of my head. "I never had ambitions to lead the masses or generations or whatever you think I will do. The fact that I got these wings over someone else with more drive is a cruel joke of the Gods. The House of Echidna's first set of wings, and they're *gifted* to me?"

Voss took a few steps away, his arms still clasped behind his currently wingless back. "Maybe Fate or the Gods saw you had nothing to live for and gifted you wings to see the possibilities laid out before you." Voss ventured across the living space, stopping at a table in the kitchen area and peering at me from over his shoulder. "If only so you would reach out and grab them."

The next morning, waking up in my cave room with stone walls and a rather hard mattress felt like I'd woken up in a prison. The clanking and hushed voices emanating from the central part of this place only amplified my isolation.

Isolation I'd battled my entire life.

Isolated from Magics who wanted to do more, be more. Isolated from my intelligent sister, despite how she was simultaneously my best friend in this whole world. Isolated from a world determined to make me into something I wasn't, to show me exactly how *different* I was from everyone else around me.

That familiar pressure pushed onto my chest, shoving my body deeper into the mattress. My mind raced, trying to fight the darkness creeping in at the corners of my mind. I cleared my dry throat, squeezing my eyes shut against the trembling that was slowly overtaking my body.

Gods, I needed to get a fucking grip.

I could use a drink, that was for sure.

I groaned obnoxiously, launching myself from the bed. After quickly throwing on casual trousers and a tunic and using the clouded mirror on the wall to comb my hair, I emerged from my seclusion and shuffled into the living space.

"So, what's on the agenda for day one?" I called as I made way for the island in the middle of the kitchen. Both sets of eyes snapped to me.

Voss leaned his hips against the counter, cradling a mug of what could be considered sludge, while Ibis narrowed his eyes at me before focusing on the breakfast on the stove.

"I have to fly into Eldamain to grab more supplies for your training," Voss explained, pushing himself off the counter. "I've placed Ibis in charge of you today, so he will give you a tour of the rest of my home and explain what may be expected of you outside of training."

"Fabulous." I grinned, my eyes glancing back to the hulking mass huddled over the stove, but he continued to ignore my existence. "Are you sure you don't need any help with the supplies?"

Voss downed the rest of his drink, placing it on the island, and cupping my shoulder as he walked toward the door. Ibis waited for Voss to leave before he snapped those golden eyes to me.

I raised my hands up in front of me, palms facing him in surrender with wide eyes and arched eyebrows. "I mean no harm in being here, but you hurt me, and I will tell Dad."

Ibis's wide lips propped open as he dramatically rolled his eyes to the back of his head. He shook those brown curls as he started to aggressively stir the grits in the pan with a death grip around the wooden spoon.

"Do you have some sort of problem with me, Ibis?" I asked, hissing at the end of his name. I strode to the edge of the island, boosting myself onto the edge where my feet dangled only inches from the ground. "I would like you to know I am here against my free will—"

"That is precisely my problem with you," Ibis snapped, that voice permeating through the air. He wheeled on me with the spoon raised between us, flinging grits onto my cheek.

I startled slightly, blinking at him and ignoring the slight sting on my cheek from the heat. His scowl fell from his face, and I waited with a sort of sick pleasure as he fought a smirk for quite some time before it went slack. Even his shoulders visibly relaxed, the look of a calmer man stirring deeper emotions within me.

I lifted a finger to my cheek, swiping the splattered food off in one sweep. I studied it briefly, then locked my gaze on Ibis's as I stuck my finger two knuckles deep into my mouth, dragging it down my tongue.

His eyes latched onto the movement, those honey hues flashing throughout.

I wiped any excess saliva on my shirt with a satisfied smirk, raising an eyebrow. "You were saying?"

Ibis gaped at me before clearing his throat and moving about the kitchen, grabbing bowls and utensils as he finished prepping breakfast. "It took me a single evening to unpack the type of person you are, *nychterída*."

"What did you just call me?" I frowned, tilting my head to the side. "Is this another old Etherean title?"

"Bat," Ibis articulated, staring at me with amusement. "It means bat."

I wanted to be mad at him for the name, especially

since Voss had already labeled me *drakon*. That name sounded more prestigious—a long-lost creature from the House of Echidna—while a *bat* just sounded…

Underwhelming.

But I was more distracted by the fact that he was convinced he'd unpacked who I was.

"And what kind of person am I, Ibis?" I placed my hands behind me on the island, reclining back a little as I subtly swung my feet.

At the sound of his name, Ibis slammed the two bowls of grits, vegetables, and cubed meat beside me. He slid in front of me and between my legs, carefully placing both hands on either side of me as he inclined his head ever so slightly to meet my gaze.

"You are crude and impertinent," Ibis sneered, scanning my face. "Despite being chosen by the Gods, you spit on their graces and defile your House name by renouncing the gift you've been given. A rare ability, may I add, that seems to answer your beck and call despite having no real training or regard for them.

"Voss is a rare Magic, and he has agreed to help you apply yourself and show the world you are more than just a pretty face." Ibis leaned in a little closer, narrowing his eyes. "But you can't be arsed."

I should've been offended by that entire monologue, but the proximity between us was doing nothing for the swirling in the pit of my stomach and the static prickling from the base of my neck to my lower back.

The corners of my lips twitched as I inched closer, leaving only an inch between us, and whispered into the air we shared, "You think I'm pretty?"

Ibis pressed his lips together, flaring his nostrils. When I tucked my bottom lip under my canine, he shoved himself away and grabbed one of the bowls of breakfast.

As he stalked off toward the living area, he threw out a quick, "Eat your food, *nychterída.*"

Chapter 3

End of Summertide 1782 A.V.

4 Months Later

The peaks looming beside us within the mountains were silent spectators to the absolute beat down I was getting from Ibis. I stood as Voss instructed, shoulder-width apart, with my left foot forward and my right foot behind me. I locked my knees with a small bend, bouncing between them to distribute my weight evenly.

After I checked my elbows to make sure they were close to my body, I glanced up. "Alright, next round—"

A hard mass collided with my jaw, a sharp pain racing across my cheek before a strange numbness took over. This time, though, my body only shifted from the impact instead of sending me sprawling to the rocky terrain beneath my feet.

I blinked past the dizziness sweeping over me, the pain only a dull, throbbing ache that matched the other side of my face.

"Son of bitch, Ibis," I grumbled while gingerly rubbing my jaw. "I wasn't even fucking ready."

"No enemy will wait until you've sat there and bounced around before they strike," Ibis lectured, stretching his arms above him like he'd just woken up.

"You must learn to tap into your Magic reflexes faster." Voss paced alongside the large, gray wall of rock, hands clasped behind his back. "It will help you to access your wings or other important gifts at the first sight of danger."

"What enemy and danger do you two expect to encounter?" I flexed my jaw, rolling it around in its socket before continuing, "You act like we're at war."

"Until you prove yourself useful to a kingdom that will give you coin to protect yourself," Ibis drawled with a scowl as he rewrapped the tape on his knuckles as if *I* messed them up intentionally. "Magics are at war every day of our lives against the kingdoms."

"My father never taught me how to fight," I explained, spreading my hands out before me. "I don't think many of the Magics in Ghita know how to fight. Clearly, they don't see every kingdom as a threat—"

"And that will be their downfall," Voss boomed, halting his stride. He twisted on the balls of his feet to face me, his tone stern. "Why do you think it is easy for the mortals to massacre entire towns of Magics at a time without consequence? Magics have spent so much time trying to hide who they are, where they are, and their gifts that they forgot to use them to their advantage. Now, we are a race of beings which does not know how to use our powers to defend ourselves."

"So, when the kingdoms *do* find us," Ibis jumped in, picking up his fighting stance again, "we cannot fight back."

I shot him a hard smile, worry prickling in the back of my mind at the thought of my father, mother, and sister entirely undefended in Ghita.

Because these two were right. Magics spent more time trying to blend in or hide their gifts, unique characteristics, and features that we forgot we were enhanced beings. If we only just taught ourselves how to fight and wield weapons, we would be unstoppable.

We wouldn't have to hide anymore.

"Again," Voss ordered, folding his arms over his chest.

I quickly took my stance and held my arms up, waiting for Ibis to deliver the first blow.

With a shake of his head and a chuckle, he went straight for my gut, but I knew my mistake had been leaving my midsection open. I blocked it with my forearm, shoving his fist away from my body. Something flickered across his gaze that lit up those golden hues as his canine peeked from under his lip and glistened in the sun.

Ibis continued to throw punch after punch, jab after jab, and I just kept deflecting as I stepped backward with every blow. The force he exerted on me was like being hit back by a wave.

As I fell into the rhythm of blocking him, I tapped into that well within me and allowed the tingling power to spread into my arms and legs. I could feel my muscles stiffen underneath my skin.

Ibis left his flank open, and I acted swiftly, rounding my arm around and nailing my fist into his side. I didn't wait to register the shock on Ibis's face because he left his entire midsection open.

Adrenaline shot through me and fueled my excitement and the power humming in my blood. My vision sharpened, and my speed intensified.

Soon, Ibis and I were dancing around one another, occasionally landing a hit on the other. My enhanced stamina kept me going as I picked up on some of Ibis's signature moves: a fake jab to the left as he brought a hook right, a swipe of his legs in an effort to take me down.

As Ibis elected for another fake maneuver, I aimed straight for his jaw and, unfortunately, felt little satisfaction as my fist connected with that chiseled line. I heard something crack, but not from within my body.

Ibis groaned at the impact, stumbling as he nearly fell to the side. My chest heaved up and down as I tried to catch my breath.

I wanted to revel in this moment, especially after having my ass handed to me by both Ibis and Voss numerous times over the last few months, but Ibis's face scrunched in pain only had me frowning.

"Well done!" Voss clapped, taking a few steps into the makeshift fighting ring. "I saw the moment you tapped into that strength, speed, and stamina. You were able to hold yourself against Ibis while you did it, too, which is impressive."

All I could do was nod as I continued to stare down at where Ibis held his palm against his jaw. The angry energy radiated off of him like the heat of a flame.

I took a step closer to Ibis, reaching out my hand between us in an effort to cool the tension thickening the air. Ibis glared at me from the corner of his eye as I shrugged, adding, "You can't win them all, right?"

Ibis suddenly lunged, tackling me to the ground in a heap of limbs. We rolled on the stone ground a few times, sharp rocks digging into my skin. As we hit the final turn, Ibis grabbed both of my arms in his hands and pinned them on the ground beside my body. He sat on top of me, straddling me so his shins dug into my thighs and his feet hooked under my knees.

My powers should have been kicking in to get me out of this situation, but my senses fixated on the flex of his muscles along my torso and his unnaturally smooth hands locked around my forearms. I honed in on the rapid rise and fall of his bronze chest, my stomach coiling as I imagined what it'd be like to have him riding me like this.

If he killed me now, I wouldn't even complain because of the view.

My body lit up from the inside out as he lowered his face dangerously close to mine, curling his lip so both of those pointed canines flashed in the daylight.

"Except me, *nychterída*." His nose almost brushed mine as he smirked. "I always win."

Chapter 4

Autumnus 1782 A.V.

2 Months Later

I followed Voss through the peaks of the Black Avalanches, weaving expertly between spires shooting up from various angles and dodging sudden walls of rock. I twisted higher into the sky to navigate above them, spinning amongst the clouds.

Since coming here six months ago, I'd come to enjoy how my wings responded to my every command. My faster reflexes even had me besting Voss in hand-to-hand combat, but I still wasn't as fast as Ibis.

Well…

I was as fast as him, but he was more skilled at it than me, with years of discipline under his proverbial belt. Apparently, he'd been learning self-defense since he was a teenager.

But flight… I wasn't necessarily outpacing Ibis and Voss, but it seemed I had more efficiency and power in my wingspan. I cut faster while still maintaining control over my flight, albeit never looking pretty. It was graceless, which was only fitting for me.

Voss headed for the nearest peak, landing soundlessly on the balls of his feet. I was right behind him, carefully plopping on the ground, my wings twitching on my back.

"Your speed is starting to match your efficiency," Voss complimented, motioning me to the edge of the cliff. "I notice you opt for exposure more often than not now."

I shrugged, sitting beside him and letting my legs hang off the ledge, the bottoms of my wings resting against the stone ground. "I want to get used to them being out more often. I've grown to like them, especially since it seems everything about them has come so naturally."

Voss stared off into the setting sun over the horizon, contemplating. "I believe your skill levels in flight will surpass Ibis's soon enough."

I thought maybe the compliment would've inflated me, but instead, it left a stale taste in my mouth. Ibis's assumption of me, that things seemed effortless, was ingrained in my brain. I definitely didn't forget the look that crossed Ibis's face last month when Voss even said something similar in front of him.

"Why is that?" I asked him, surveying his facial expression. As always, Voss never gave away what he was thinking if he didn't want you to know. "You and Ibis have made side comments that it seems my gifts come quickly to me compared to him. Why would that be?"

"I asked myself this very question when my own gifts emerged," Voss sighed heavily, squinting. "When I met the Great Karasi, I again asked how Magics varied so drastically over the centuries. There is another Magic who resides in Mariande who has a century on me, and he is of the House of Argo."

"I've heard of him." I perked up, feeling dignified for once that I knew something about our kind. "He can speak the water language."

"That is correct." Voss nodded. He peeked at me from the corners of his eyes, tapping two fingers to his neck. "Scales run up and down his body in sporadic patches, and his eyes swirl with the ocean."

"And I thought purple was cool," I grumbled under my breath, but Voss just glared at me. "Have you been able to come to a conclusion or a best guess as to why our powers are the way they are?"

Voss quietly contemplated, or at least I thought that's what the look on his face always meant. Barely opening his mouth, he asked, "What do you know of our history, boy? And I mean the long history."

"It's vague." I brushed some gravel from my hands. I let my shoulders hunch forward. "When the Gods first created the mortals and the Sirians, Morana also created the mythical beings that used to roam Aveesh. I don't know much about them, but you have mentioned the *drakon*.

"But the Gods wanted to talk with the beings, to understand how they worked, so Morana merged their bodies with mortal souls. When she did that, they were given the ability to switch between mortal and animal form."

"That is all that we know of our mythology," Voss explained with another heavy sigh as if the weight of our existence rested on his shoulders. "We aren't sure why we've lost the ability to fully shift into animals over time, or when that all stopped, but much like the rest of the world, we believe it always had something to do with the Gods leaving our world."

"Some people say the Gods left our world when King Korbin essentially got rid of the Sirians. How true do you think that is?"

Voss smirked to himself, shaking his head. "I think the Gods left us long before that, even if their demi-god children still roamed Aveesh."

I recalled my mother talking about the demi-gods... "If the

Houses of Magics were founded by demi-gods, do you think they were able to shift into full animals?"

"They were able to shift between animal and mortal form," Voss confirmed, bending his knee and resting his forearm on top of it. "You do not know of the mythical forms of the Houses?"

I shook my head, which had him rubbing at the light spattering of scruff along his chin.

"Each House was associated with two to three mythological beings, none of which have been translated into our modern language. How can we when there is nothing to give names to?"

Voss began listing them on his fingers as he went through each. "The House of Echidna had the *drakon* and the *thirio*. The *drakon* were winged beasts with skin like a snake's. They were shaped like lizards, but their sizes were incomparable, their adult forms nearly as big as the peaks surrounding us. The *thirio* looked just like a lizard, but the size of an elephant and the ability to walk on its hind legs."

He gestured toward the lake below us. "The House of Argo had the *nereids* and *ketea*. The *nereids* were half-fish and half-mortal, with one long tailfin in place of their legs. The *ketea* were like the *drakon*, but they lurked within the water and could not survive on land."

I tried to picture a world where not only Magics shifted into these creatures I only envisioned in nightmares, but a world where it was just mortals and Sirians living amongst these beings without the ability to communicate.

If the tales are to be believed.

How different would our world be if Magics could shift into a *drakon* or *ketea*? It would be damn near impossible for mortals to ignore us then.

"The House of Nemea was gifted with three mythological

beings." Voss now held up three fingers between us. "The *lycan, gryps,* and *hippogryph.* The *lycan* were large wolves that rivaled those within The Overgrowns, nearly triple their size. *Gryps* were half-lion and half-eagle while the *hippogryphs* were half-eagle and half-horse."

"Which halves were which?" I asked, wincing.

Voss wiggled his eyebrows at me with a shrug. "Who knows? Either way, they both were gifted flight, which is why Ibis and I have feathered wings that vary in hue."

My head wanted to explode. So many images flashed across my brain at this history lesson, from Ibis shifting into a strange half-bird animal to what it would feel like for my whole body to shift into this *drakon* that Voss spoke of.

As dusk started to absorb all the light in the sky, I wheeled my gaze on Voss. "Shouldn't we head back? It's getting dark out."

"A final test for the evening." Voss smiled, twisting to face me. "Let us see if you have the night vision that comes from your House."

"Right now?" I clamored to my feet, sweeping my arms around us. "While we're on top of a *mountain,* you want to test if I have night vision?"

"Incentive." Not this again… An eerie smirk climbed up Voss's cheeks. "I do not have night vision, as it is not granted to my House. You, though, could possibly have it, thus being the only way we are getting home tonight. Otherwise, we'll be left to battle whatever may lurk within these peaks at night."

"You've gotta be fucking kidding me," I groaned, throwing my head up to the sky. "You know, this whole life or death incentive thing is starting to get really old."

But Voss didn't budge, just squinted toward the horizon as the sun winked out for the day.

As it plunged us into a deep, endless night, my hearing took control over my senses.

Small animals scurried across loose rocks, something most definitely *dragged* across the stone, and wings rustled nearby. Not Voss nor I, but somewhere within another peak.

"You brought Ibis out here?" I snapped, not sure whether I should be irritated or feel pity that Ibis might have heard Voss's earlier comment about me surpassing him.

"Another incentive." I could hear Voss's clothes shift as he probably shrugged his shoulders. "One more helpless Magic trapped on this mountain unless you're able to lead us out."

I ground my teeth, trying to calm my racing heart and overstimulated brain, attempting to make sense of all the sounds of the night.

"How do I..." I trailed off, squeezing my eyes shut. "Turn it on?"

"You're telling me you don't know how to turn something on, *nychterída*?" Ibis's voice traveled across the rocky plane, wrapping around me. A smirk twitched at the corner of my lips as I instinctively took a blind step forward.

I didn't take another, considering I no longer knew where the ledge was.

"Oh, bird boy," I chuckled, rubbing my palms down my thighs. "I know plenty about the body to know—"

"Concentrate, Remiel," Voss growled, agitation evident in his tone. "I would like to be back in the confines of my home."

"Scared of the dark, boss?" I laughed again at my own joke, and I could *feel* Ibis rolling his eyes. "No one forced you to test me out here."

I knew I had to open my eyes to activate this night vision but opening them to the endless dark was more intense than the back of my eyelids. Outside of the animals and bugs inhabiting the Avalanches, the night seemed to pulse around me, imperceptible waves of black fluttering at the corners of my eyes as my natural vision willed itself to latch onto something—anything.

I reached down into the well within myself, where the wings disappeared when I folded them away, digging around for some sort of indication that I had power within to see into the darkness.

I listened to my body and that power, struggling to pinpoint where I felt a new sensation I could listen to or that was asking for me to focus on—

There. In the middle of my head, behind my eyes, where I would assume they connected to my brain, there was an energy tingling the nerves in my mind. I inhaled, my chest expanding as I reached for that fizzling that begged me to pay attention to my body.

With my hand inside the well, I shoved the power through my veins, buzzing into my head as a jolt of energy pulsed in my eyes. Tears sprung to the corners and leaked over my lids as I doubled over with a grunt.

Someone shuffled their feet, but I was too awed at the shift in my vision to know if it was Voss or Ibis.

Slowly, the more I blinked, the more my feet started to appear in my vision, and the ground I stood on came into focus. I gradually lifted myself back to full height, nearly jumping off the cliff behind me as my vision continued to adjust.

My surroundings looked exactly the same as they did in daylight, although the edges of the mountain peaks and Voss's body beside me were slightly blurred around the edges like I was looking at them through an opaque, green-hued glass.

"Remiel?" Ibis called to my right, and I twirled my head in the direction of his voice. Standing between two peaks, his legs were planted one in front of the other with a hand outstretched as he blindly stared into the dark. His wings twitched on his back, no longer their pure white but green within my vision.

I took slow, steady footsteps toward Ibis, admiring his cut jawline and the strong swell of his chest while he couldn't see me doing so. As I neared, he repositioned himself so he was standing alarmingly still with his hands at his sides, staring off over my shoulder.

I carefully reached for his forearm, brushing my fingers along a vein. Even in the dark with this strange hue, our skin tones still drastically contrasted with one another. He twitched at my touch, and I wondered if he'd become accustomed to it from all the hand-to-hand combat.

I leaned into him, gently inhaling his warmth as I placed my cheek against his, whispering, "The sound of my name on your lips is a high I will never concede."

He lurched back, snarling at where I stood, and I couldn't fight the giggle that fell from my lips.

"Something tells me that you've accessed the night vision," Voss called, and I turned to see him rolling his eyes. "And the first thing you choose to do is harass your peer."

"It's nice to have an upper hand for once," I grumbled under my breath, but I swore I caught a tick in Ibis's cheek.

"Well, lead the way back to our cave, Remiel," Voss commanded as he slipped the thick rope from off his belt and held the end of it out for me to take. I stretched it toward Ibis, our fingers brushing as he took it from me. "You continue to amaze me, *drakon*. Nearly six months with your unique gifts, and you've all but mastered calling them to you, even those you didn't know existed."

Ibis stiffened beside me. Out of the corner of my eye, I saw him clench his jaw, and his grip tightened around the rope.

"Another six months, and I expect you to be fully caught up with Ibis."

Before we took flight, I watched with no satisfaction as Ibis's shoulders deflated and he cast his head toward the ground.

Chapter 5

Midwinter 1783 A.V.

4 Months Later

Ibis cleaned up breakfast in the kitchen as I sat in front of the fire in the middle of the living space, whipping up a few different potions at Voss's request. Apparently, neither of them knew anything about potions since it was the *women's* jobs where they had come from.

Well, in Voss's case, *when* he was born.

I chuckled to myself at the absurdity of that statement, especially considering we were all gifted with the blood used to enhance the potions in the first place. I wanted to write to Cara and tell her about it, especially because I could just see the pure outrage lighting up those purple eyes and the earful she'd give to either of them for that belief.

But then I remembered Voss's decree on not sending notes home to avoid *unnecessary distraction*, and frustration bubbled in my chest.

I tried to keep my eyes on my work, grinding the perilla leaf and chamomile into a powder as the aloe simmered on the fire. I reached for the spatula to give it a quick stir when Voss emerged from the hallway he and Ibis shared.

"I have business to attend to for the day," Voss announced, tightening his fur cloak around his neck and waist. I almost busted out laughing at the cap he wore, a thick leather with flaps that covered his ears and tied under his chin, lined with more fur.

"Will you need help?" Ibis asked, his arms submerged in the wash basin.

Voss pursed his lips, shaking his head. "I will be venturing into The Clips today, so no need to fret. You two can stay here and... entertain one another, I suppose."

I shot a mischievous smile Ibis's way, and I took great pleasure in the way he set his jaw and flared his nostrils at me in response.

"You can't be serious," Ibis grumbled, still glaring at me. I huffed under my breath as I stirred the aloe to prevent it from burning.

"Quite serious." Voss strolled across the room, pausing at the door to furl his hand in my direction. "In fact, Ibis, I believe you would benefit from being Remiel's student for once."

"Excuse me?" Ibis gawked at the same time I choked on my own spit. Ibis ignored me as he pressed further, "I'm not sure I have much to learn from the bat boy."

"Says the bird boy," I mocked under my breath, but we all knew our hearing was enhanced enough to hear me.

"On the contrary," Voss said, pulling the door open, a rush of cold air nearly blowing the fire out. I curled my wing to block it, and it was my turn to glare at Voss. "Remiel is rather skilled in potions and elixirs, and that is something we could all benefit from learning." He turned his gaze on me then, instructing, "Teach Ibis how to make the potions you're working on today."

I nodded once because what else was I supposed to say? *No?*

In reality, I felt joy in being able to order Ibis around for once and lend him my knowledge on something he didn't know.

With that, Voss slammed the door shut behind him and left me alone with Ibis for the second time since I arrived ten months ago. I slid my wing back behind me, letting the bottom rest against the ground.

"Come join me, bird boy," I called from my spot on the ground, beckoning him with a wave.

He stood facing me with his fists clenched at his side, still dripping from the wash basin. A solid minute passed before he groaned, wiped his hands on a towel, and trekked across the room to sit in the leather chair beside me.

He raised an eyebrow at me, waving his hand over the pot and the fire.

I cleared my throat, watching the flames dance beneath the pot. I wasn't sure where to start, and Ibis staring at me not-so-patiently had my stomach twisting in a knot. The pressure on my chest intensified, and I frowned because I never had this sort of anxiety helping Cara with potions.

My heart clenched at the thought of my sister, and I wondered if I would drop dead from the tightness in my chest cavity.

"I don't have all day, *nychterída*," Ibis sighed, leaning back against the chair.

That snapped me out of my spiral, and I smirked up at him. "It's freezing outside. We are effectively trapped here—have been for months—and you're telling me you have something better to be doing?"

Ibis didn't respond but glowered at me.

"Voss is right, you know," I began, handing him the spatula. He took it without hesitation, holding it like he was ready to flip something. "Adding healing knowledge and basic potions mastery to your repertoire could give you an advantage in a kingdom."

"My repertoire?" Ibis questioned, curling a lip.

I rolled my eyes and pointed at the pot. "This is aloe vera. I believe you're familiar with the aloe plant?"

"It grows in Riddling," Ibis grumbled, staring at the chunky liquid.

"Well, it has a lot of uses," I explained, muddling the plants in my mortar. "When pulled from the plant, the jelly can be applied directly to burns, reddened skin, dry skin, and wounds. It has great healing properties."

"So why are you cooking it?" Ibis side-eyed me before peering into the pot.

"It makes it easier to digest and sometimes mix with other potions and salves." I observed him as he cautiously stirred the aloe in the pot, then raised an eyebrow at me in question. I nodded, trying to suppress my grin. "Like cooking, don't let it burn or boil. Just let it simmer."

That comparison seemed to loosen the tension from his shoulders as they drooped, and he relaxed against the chair. Despite the visceral release though, I still sensed his guard up, walls placed between us for whatever reason.

"And what are you doing there?" Ibis pointed at the pestle and mortar in my hand.

"Grinding up herbs that can be used for teas, patching wounds, or mixed in with an elixir." I pointed at the two bowls of plants I still had, elaborating, "The perilla leaf can help with respiratory illnesses like a common cold or breathing problem. It can also help with pain. The chamomile has many benefits, depending on what you mix it with. Stomach issues, sores, mental blockades… The likes."

Ibis just nodded as his eyes bounced from the bowls to the mortar in my hand and back to the aloe in the pot. Again, he pointed at it with inquiry. "What do we do when it's done? And how do we know it's done?"

"When most of the chunks have dissolved, we'll strain it into a jar and let it cool off."

Ibis slowly dragged his gaze back to me. His eyes narrowed skeptically as though he were debating whether or not everything I said was true.

I chuckled, dumping the ground herbs into a tin and adding more fresh plants into the mortar. "You may think I'm trying to sabotage your learning, but I promise, Ibis, it is not that serious."

"To you, it might not be," Ibis said, frowning. "But my position as an apprentice is very serious to me. Have you ever considered Voss may need to choose between us when a kingdom asks for his endorsement? You already have an upper hand over me if you continue to develop more skills from your House while learning how to utilize them effectively. Now, you know how to make potions. Teaching me to do so would put us on even footing."

I dropped the pestle and mortar into my lap, my hands limp around them. "You're so fucking serious sometimes it's exhausting. I couldn't care less about whatever rivalry you think exists between us."

"I don't *think* it does." Ibis paused, leaning forward with his forearms braced on his thighs. "I *know* it does. Voss has something to say to you any time you come up with a new trick, especially when you seem to wield it like you've been doing so all your life."

"I can't change what someone thinks about me," I scoffed, throwing my hands out. "What do you want me to tell Voss? 'Pay more attention to your other child because he yearns for Daddy's validation more than I do'?"

I regretted the words the moment they left my lips, wincing.

But they had already been said, and Ibis's face drew tight in anger, every muscle taught. He slowly inhaled as he ground his teeth, his shoulders lifting with the breath. He lurched from his seat in a moment and reached across the space between us to grab me by the collar of my shirt. He dragged me from the ground as he rose, hauling me against him.

Common sense tried to tell me I should be ready for a fight, but instead, my body hummed in anticipation.

Heavy breaths mingling, I smirked as I said quietly, "You know when Voss said to entertain each other, this is *exactly* what I had in mind."

Ibis growled, and I had to conjure pure thoughts as I battled with my cock, pleading for it to stand down. He threw me away from him onto the couch behind me with an angry stare pointed my way.

Without another word, he marched to his room and slammed the door behind him, and I swore the cave shuddered at the strength he put into it.

⁂

The next morning, I emerged from my room to Voss returning home. He gave me a quick nod of his head before he rushed into his room, calling out over his shoulder, "Eat some breakfast before we train inside today. I will quickly bathe myself."

I pressed my lips together into a tight grin as Ibis mumbled an acknowledgment from the kitchen. My heart stopped in my chest as I peered at him from the corner of my eyes, his back turned to me.

He hadn't emerged from his room during the rest of the day before except to silently cook himself lunch and dinner, not even bothering to offer me any.

But I didn't blame him. I might have pushed a line there with the validation comment. I vaguely knew his ambitions were directly aligned with what Voss wanted for us, and as far as I let on, I had no interest in working for any kingdom.

Which was true.

I suspired as I dragged myself to the kitchen to grab a simple slice of bread and banana, but when I approached the island, Ibis slowly slid a bowl of oats and cured meat across it.

Without meeting my eye, he mumbled, "Sorry."

I startled, gawking at him. "What the fuck are you sorry for?"

"I lost my temper yesterday, and you didn't deserve that." He placed his own bowl on the counter beside him, lifting those beautiful eyes to mine. "You were only doing what Voss told you to, and I let my jealousy get the better of me. For that, I apologize."

"Well, thank you?" I pulled the bowl closer to me on the opposite side of the island, shaking my head. "But it's really unnecessary. I should apologize for what I said. It wasn't fair—"

"We'll call it even." He nodded, but there was a strange expression on his face as if he were attempting to read me.

I chuckled, stirring my oats with a raised eyebrow. "Something else on your mind, bird boy?"

"I had quite a bit of alone time yesterday to do some thinking," Ibis explained, folding his arms across his broad chest as he leaned back against the counter. The tunic he wore strained across the swell of his muscles. "Your application to your herbs is contradictory to what I've come to know about you."

"You think I'm stupid?" I laughed, throwing my head back.

"Not stupid, per se." Ibis pursed his lips, cocking his head. "You're very flippant about most things, but it seems with potions, you have a serious, studious quality to you for once. Like you're actually enjoying what you're doing, and you apply yourself."

"Trust me, you think you know who I am," I said, my voice low as I scooped up some oats. "But you don't know the first thing about me."

Ibis's silence only made me squirm, and his observation of me looped in my head repeatedly as he started to eat.

Not stupid, but flippant. I'd been told that so many times in my life since I was a young kid. Most people I'd encountered in Ghita didn't know how much I contributed to my father's apothecary because I spent every single night at a pub or in another's bed.

"Contradictory," I mumbled around my food before swallowing, "I would say that's the best way to explain who I am."

Ibis didn't respond or goad, but I felt his stare searing into the side of my head. More so, I felt those walls around him, and I wondered why they were there.

I thought about why I kept my own walls up, why I didn't let those I thought were friends in Ghita see that *studious* quality Ibis saw, the more serious side of me.

I cleared my throat, placing my bowl down. "It's ironic that as Magics, we are different. Different from mortals, but also different from Sirians. We can live in the world, but only if we stay quiet and hidden with our heads down…"

I slowly lifted my head to look at Ibis through my lashes, his face drawn tight. "Do you know what it's like to be different from those who are already different?"

Something foreign flashed across his eyes, and I grabbed onto that fleeting emotion I rarely saw.

"I have always been too different for Magics, for my father…" I bit against the nerves trembling through me. "I've never had ambition to do much of anything in my life, yet I was skilled at potions. It didn't help me any that my sister was considered the studious one of the two of us, so people wanted to give her that label. Because I didn't talk about owning my own apothecary or greenhouse, people assumed that the dream wasn't there. They never saw me working for my father. All they saw me do was drink at the pubs and gallivant about the town. How could I be both?

"People even applied it to my love life, as if it were anyone's business what I did behind closed doors." I could never forget the look on people's faces when I told them I enjoyed both men and women—and anything in between. "Because I enjoyed the company of all, it confused people. How could I love *both*? And, because I loved both, to them it meant I would never pick just one person to have and love for the rest of my life. I would forever be too different to have a family…"

I swallowed against the memory and emotions that tickled my throat. Cara had laid with me the entire night after the encounter.

I cleared my throat. "How would I explain to my future children that daddy enjoys men, or explain to them that daddy also loves women, but I adopted them because I wanted to spend my life with a man? People wanted me to only pick one, otherwise it was too confusing for them."

Ibis's face gradually softened during my little speech, his arms falling limp at his sides.

And Gods, I forgot how fucking beautiful he was, the light bouncing off those brown ringlets that clung tight to his head and making his golden skin glow.

I shook the emotions out of my head. "Being a contradictory individual and too different is very isolating," I quietly admitted.

Ibis's head twitched imperceptibly as he blinked rapidly. He opened and closed his mouth a few times before actually saying, "Why are you telling me this?"

My heart clenched in my chest at the walls still fortified around him, but I wasn't about to back down. "Because I get what it's like to have to fight to prove yourself. To prove that you can belong somewhere. And to show you that things have not always come easily to me in life as you may believe."

At that moment, Voss entered the living room with a clap of his hands. "Let's start the day with some training."

I patted the top of the wooden island before joining Voss in the space between the living area and kitchen, helping him scoot the chairs and couch around the firepit like a blockade. By the time we'd created a decent opening in the middle of the cave, Ibis finally joined us in the space.

"You two know what to do." Voss waved his hand in the space. "I am too tired to get you two to try anything new, so how about… Don't hold back."

I was usually able to hold myself against Ibis, but that statement had a weight dropping to the pit of my stomach. Especially considering the anger I'd elicited from Ibis yesterday, apology or not. If I'd learned anything from that small tantrum, it was that Ibis had something to prove.

Which is why he didn't hesitate when he closed the space between us and sent a fist straight into the middle of my face without warning.

"Fucking shit, Ibis," I hissed, cupping my nose in my hand, which was definitely broken. But he didn't let up. He kept coming for me, landing blows on my torso and arms that were sure to leave dark bruises.

"Come on, Remiel," Voss called nonchalantly with a hint of disappointment. "You can recall faster than that. Fight back."

"Just give me a second," I mumbled around the blood dripping down my face, spitting some of it onto the floor.

Ibis just smirked as he hooked his arm and landed a blow to my ribs, and I heard a snap.

Blinding pain flashed in my eyes as I doubled over, falling to my hands and knees on the ground. I coughed around the pain, blood dripping onto the stone underneath me.

"Don't bleed on the floor, *nychterída*," Ibis growled under his breath. I peeked from the side where he bounced on the balls of his feet, unscathed.

"Do you yield, then?" Voss sighed, his disappointment hanging in the air. "That fast?"

I growled in frustration, not so much at the disappointment from Voss as the betrayal I felt. After he'd apologized, after I opened up to him more than I'd opened up to anyone besides Cara…

The burning in my chest amplified, spreading through my body.

I grunted as I rose from my knees, favoring my right side where Ibis had surely broken my rib. I hissed as I uncurled from the hunch, a hand held up between us. At first, Ibis hesitated, his gaze flashing from my hand outstretched to where the other clutched my side. There was even a moment I thought regret dimmed his eyes.

But just as quickly as I saw it, he lunged for me again, and I saw red.

I removed my hand from my side, and I don't know what came over me. All I remembered was my fingers tingling before I registered a sharp stinging at the nailbeds.

I ignored it as I swiped my hand across the space between Ibis and me, and he dodged my hand just in time to miss my attack.

"Claws," Voss huffed in disbelief, shaking his head with a wide grin. "You also have retractable claws."

I stared down at my right fingers, which were coated in blood, but pointed talons protruded from where my nails used to be. They curved slightly at the ends and were thicker and denser. I felt their weight as I held them in front of me like a foreign object.

"At this rate, you're one step away from shifting into a full *drakon*." Voss walked up beside me, but my attention went to Ibis, remembering the conversation from yesterday. Shock warred on his face with astonishment. "Good on you for retreating, Ibis. He could've done some damage with those."

Cold terror swept over me then, settling into my skin.

I had never lost my temper, not really. At that moment, I was so hurt and angry that I'd unintentionally brought forth a deadly weapon.

I didn't linger long on that feeling because, while I was still mortified at almost seriously injuring Ibis, I still felt my own aching rib from where he'd broken it.

The look on his face when we locked eyes would be branded in my brain for the rest of my life because that was betrayal that morphed his features into a deep frown.

We were, indeed, even again.

Chapter 6

Springtide 1783 A.V.

2 Months Later

The house before me hadn't changed in the slightest, as if a year hadn't passed since the last time I stood before our wooden door. At the same time, it'd only been a *year*, and yet it felt like a lifetime ago. I glanced over my shoulder at the tree where Cara and I discussed romantics the night before I left.

Gods, it'd only been a *year*?

"Remy?" Cara's voice shouted from somewhere within the house. Shortly after that, the door burst open, and a smile sprung to my face at the sight of my little sister standing in the doorway, one hand limp at her side and the other poised on the doorknob.

"Hey, Cee," I barely managed, fighting the emotion clogging my throat. She sprinted down the steps and across the lawn, then flung herself into my arms. She clung to my neck as she buried her head into my chest.

Tears burned the corners of my eyes as the scent of her rose soap filled my nose, and the ache in my chest any time I thought of her was amplified now that she was in my arms.

"Let me look at you," she giggled around her own tears, quickly brushing them away. She held me at arms-length, barely inclining her head to look at me.

"Look at me?" I squealed, grabbing her biceps so our arms locked between us. "Cee, you've grown taller in a year! What in the Gods?"

That wasn't the only thing different about her, either. I knew the ages between fourteen and eighteen brought about great changes for mortals, Magics, and Sirians alike, but Cee looked so mature.

She was nearly six feet tall by this point, with a long, lean body like our mother and me. She still had the same button nose as us too, but her face had thinned, accenting those cheekbones and chin giving her more pointed features like our mother where I resembled our father.

"You look healthier," Cara whispered softly, unlatching her hand from my arm to cup my now-stubbled cheek. "And since when did you keep your facial hair?"

I shrugged, but her comment about me being healthier hit me square in the chest. Training with Ibis every single day and testing my innate strength must have caught up, but no matter how much I tried, my Magic strength wasn't visible like his. I still looked lean compared to him and his sculpted muscles.

"Remiel?" My mother's singsong voice carried all the way to us, and a tear carved a path down my cheek.

Cara pulled away to reveal our mother standing on the edge of the porch with a towel clenched in one hand and her other clutching her chest. I cupped Cara's cheek, shooting her a wink before making my way to the house.

Standing at the bottom of the porch, Mother threw herself into my arms, similarly to Cara, except she was still a whole foot shorter than me. She gripped my shoulders, planting kiss after kiss on my cheek.

"Mother, look at him," Cara interrupted from behind us as I gently placed her back on the ground. Cara saddled up beside her, looping their arms together as Cara swung her free hand up and down my body. "It's like a new-and-improved, adult Remy has replaced our beloved Remiel. A man stands before you now."

"Would you stop?" I chuckled, giving her shoulder a shove. "I'm still me."

Mother offered a kind, soft smile, cupping my cheek like Cara had on the lawn. "You are still my bright star, even if you do look… so, very well."

Tears rimmed her already wet eyes, piercing my heart, so I yanked them under my arms and tucked Mother's head underneath my chin.

"Did somebody use *adult* and *Remy* in the same sentence?" Father's voice called from inside the house. Mother, Cara, and I detached before following single file under the threshold, the smell of warm, baked bread smacking me in the face.

"And side by side," Cara chided, resting her hips against the back of the couch as she crossed her arms over her chest, still studying me.

Father rose from his place at the table, twisting to face me. When he beheld me, the flash in his eyes was definitely shock at first, but it turned softer as a slow smile crept up the corners of his lips, pulling that mustache with it.

"A fine man indeed," Father agreed with a nod, extending his hand out between us.

I gave it a sidelong glance before accepting it and tapping into that Magic well to squeeze a little tighter than I normally would. His eyes flared wide as he stared down at where our hands were still clasped, and then he tugged me into a rare hug.

"It's good to see you, son," Father mumbled against the side of my face, patting my shoulder. "I want to hear all about what you have been doing and how your apprenticeship has progressed."

"You mean my *co*-apprenticeship?" Father gripped my shoulders, holding me in front of him with a frown on his face. I elaborated, "Voss already had another Magic apprentice when I got there. He's been with him for about three years now."

"Voss did not mention..." Father's frown deepened as he squinted at me, tilting his head to the side. "Please, sit down. Viella, Cara—join us."

Cara galloped across the floor, sliding into the chair beside Father's as I took my usual spot across from her. Mother brought fresh bread and homemade jam to the table, placing it in the middle as she slowly lowered to the seat across from Father.

"First, I want to hear about this *co-apprenticeship*." Father curled his lip imperceptibly at the word. "What does it mean for you?"

"I don't think it's really meant much," I explained, shrugging as I gnawed at my bottom lip. "I mean, Voss hasn't outright said that he's going to endorse one guy over the other. But, in ways, he has sort of pinned us against each other indirectly... If that makes sense."

"He might have you both under him, but he's still going to pick favorites," Cara said, leaning back into the wooden chair. "So, what's this other apprentice like? Does he hail from Echidna, too?"

I chuckled darkly at that; those golden eyes flashed in my head. "Neither of them do. They're both from the House of Nemea. His name is Ibis, and he's from Riddling."

"That sounds like a problem, them being from the same house," Cara pressed, raising an eyebrow.

"Cara," Father warned, but I waved him away.

"Voss is actually great at the—" I paused, considering my words. In reality, Voss would boast about something Ibis could do, and then he'd test me to see if I could do it or the equivalent for my House. It usually only took me a few tries to produce a result, which is what really fascinated Voss. "It doesn't cause a problem. He seems to be amused by my abilities and the knack I have for controlling or mastering them."

But what amused Voss only pissed off Ibis or got to him on some level that had him retreating internally or to his room.

"Now, that is something I'm more interested in." Father clapped, rubbing his hands together as he grinned playfully. "You said abilities? Multiple?"

I tried to suppress the smile and fluttering in my chest, but the pride written across my father's face was something I never thought I'd see.

So, I divulged everything I had learned and went through the entirety of the last year.

I told them about my wings and how I mastered not only calling them to me but also utilizing them to fly faster and with more precision. When I told them about my night vision, they went ballistic about how special it was to see in the dark. The most recent development with my retractable claws intrigued Cara, especially as I went into detail about how they shot out from my nail beds like a second set of nails.

The initial pain was still as visceral as my terror in the moment when I finally realized why Father had wanted me to learn and control any gifts I acquired from our Echidna lineage.

I tried to play off that I had even more enhanced strength, stamina, and other enhanced abilities just like them. In Voss fashion, I hypothesized they probably had the same levels I did and had just never tapped into it before. From there, Cara insisted I teach her how to channel them so she could show others in Ghita.

And when she told me that, it hit something deep inside me.

It was like finding a missing piece to a puzzle needed to continue the masterpiece.

After dinner with my family, I scooped Cara into my arms and flew with her to Ghita's main square, hovering above our town as the people stopped and ogled. We heard their voices float from below, awed at the wings and my honed skill at not only flying but being able to carry someone with me.

When I gently dropped into the square, Cara scrambled excitedly from my arms and towards a few of her friends who had been there. Plenty of others I knew from childhood and my many exploits in town also flocked around me, asking how my apprenticeship was going and marveling at how different I looked.

Everyone kept saying how healthy I was—glowing from the inside out, shining like a star—and yet I didn't feel all that different.

Although, I definitely looked at the town square through a different lens.

Instead of seeing people I'd been completely obliterated with, those I'd fooled around with in dark allies or in pub bathrooms, I saw helpless, defenseless Magics who had no idea the kind of power running in their veins. I thought about training Cara to tap into her own well while Mother and Father cooked dinner earlier.

It didn't take her long to find it and land a punch that knocked the wind out of me. She even kept up with me as we raced across the lawn, neither of us winded despite how far and fast we'd gone.

This only made me wonder how many Magics had an unknown strength within them despite the characteristics they may or may not have.

As I shook numerous hands and clapped the backs of former lovers and friends, smiling at how incredible it felt to learn how to use my gifts, I pondered if working for a kingdom was actually my calling at all.

I wasn't sure Voss would respond kindly to my not wanting to work with the kingdoms but rather with towns like Ghita which were ripe with Magics and ready to be picked off by said kingdoms.

"As much as I *loved* flying," Cara said, interrupting my thoughts, "let's go walk through town. I want to hear everything about this Ibis because you can't hide anything from me."

I looped her hand through the crook of my arm and rested my own hand on top. She guided us down the streets, past shops, restaurants, and pubs and I found myself turning my head from them without any desire to drop in.

"So, he's from Riddling?" Cara began, side-eyeing me. "Tell me more! What's he like?"

"If you could conjure a man who is opposite of me in every sense of the word, that is Ibis."

"Opposites always attract." She wiggled her eyebrows as she bumped our shoulders together. "Go on. Don't hold back."

What was there to say about Ibis?

Painfully beautiful, tough like steel, as serious as a funeral, and yet he radiated warmth. We spent every waking moment in the same vicinity, either going about our chores in a comfortable silence or taunting one another in the fighting ring. While my teasing was always laced with profanities, flirtations, and maybe some crudeness, he was always so critical and harsh.

Nothing I couldn't handle, though.

"He's incredibly ambitious," I began, staring ahead of us as children ran across the sidewalk in front of us. "He has the same mindset as Voss—that we're in a unique position with our gifts to be favored by the kingdoms, and we can use that to our advantage. But they are both closed off about it. Despite living with them in close proximity for a year, I feel like I barely know anything about either one of them."

"You don't have to know someone's entire past or every minute detail to care for them." Cara pursed her lips, tilting her head to the side. "Consider yourself, Remy. I've loved every version of you. I may not actually know this version of you and everything of the last year, but I still know your soul. This Ibis could be different from the Ibis he was before he started apprenticing with Voss, but it doesn't mean you don't *know* him."

I glared at my sister, curling my lip. "When the fuck did you get wise?"

"You once insisted you were the romantic of the two of us." She placed her free hand on top of mine that rested on hers, sandwiching it as she patted it. "Just because you've slept with half the town doesn't mean you know what romance is, brother."

"Ouch, Cee." But I smiled, nonetheless.

We walked in silence, letting the music sneaking out from the pubs wrap around us. It was a familiar and nostalgic embrace for me, but I did not find the same solace in it as I once did.

Everything really had changed for me. It seemed that maybe my purpose was slowly unfolding before me, even if I didn't know all the technicalities of how I would achieve what I wanted or confront Voss about it. Besides, I still had who knows how long with him as an apprentice, so I could always learn everything I needed to before I started on my own mission.

But I couldn't help the deep twisting in my gut at the thought of Ibis and me existing separately outside the walls of that cave.

"You have a lot more on your mind than you normally do." Cara stopped walking. "What's going on? You used to tell me everything without hesitation."

I considered for a moment, watching the townspeople scurry about over her shoulder. "Voss has expressed that living a solitary life is important to the work we may do one day. To have any ties to people is a weakness... But when I think about the work I want to do, how I want to use my gifts, it's not exactly what he'd condone."

"You don't have to do what he says, Remy," Cara said quietly, slipping her hand into mine. "You don't have to do what either of them says."

"I know that," I assured her with a nod, "but when I think about leaving Ibis behind, turning our backs on one another when the time comes..."

My heart clenched again, the anxiousness similar to how I felt leaving home a year ago, leaving Cara behind.

"Oh, Remiel," Cara snickered in disbelief, shaking her head at me. "You've fallen for your co-apprentice?"

I startled, meeting her identical purple eyes, now glistening in the glow of the streetlamps. "What?"

"You are in love with him," Cara said, softer this time, giving my hand a squeeze. She smirked as she added, "You don't have to know everything about someone to know you love who they are."

I was frozen in place, my mouth agape like a fish. I hadn't considered love between us because I always knew he wouldn't love me back. He'd made his feelings towards me very clear from the beginning.

But I guess unrequited love was what the poets wrote about.

She laughed at my stunned expression, resuming our walk through the streets hand-in-hand. I eventually shut my mouth and continued to stare down the alleys we passed, thinking about Ibis and how I felt like my existence was orbiting him like a planet around a sun.

When we passed a particularly shaded alleyway, I slowed my pace as I caught a few men huddled together, talking amongst themselves. I waited until they were nearly out of eyesight when I stopped walking altogether, hushing Cara before she could say anything.

I tried to listen to what they were saying, tapping into my enhanced hearing and amplifying my vision a tad, but there were way too many other noises assaulting my ears, from the chatter of closer patrons to the music blaring around us.

All I could see was them talking together and glancing over their shoulders, miming some strange hand gestures that were stiff and appeared rehearsed. They pointed flattened hands up and down the alleyways, swinging like pendulums, an occasional quick flick of their wrists. It seemed like a code or language they all understood, but I wasn't familiar with it.

"Remy?" Cara asked quietly, jabbing my side. "What is it?"

Something in my gut swirled uncharacteristically as the base of my neck prickled. One of the men in the group quickly turned their head toward me as he spoke, which allowed me to at least catch what he said as his mouth moved.

Plan.

My ears picked up the faintest accent, but all I could tell was it sounded Etherean, which meant they were from Mariande or Etherea.

But people from Mariande and Etherea never ventured outside of their country, not to The Clips at least.

Unless they were here on business.

"Come on," I told her, shaking the thought from my head. I guided her back the way we came. "They look like they might be up to no good."

"Did you hear them?" Cara shot her head over her shoulder, trying to gain a better look. I yanked her forward, though, determined to get her away from their eyes.

"Not really." I huddled closer into her, occasionally glancing back to make sure we weren't being followed. "They sounded like they were from Mariande or Etherea."

"There have been some Ethereans here recently," Cara explained, shrugging. "Just some knights passing through, though. They said they had been doing some business with The Clips or something."

"How do you know this?" I asked, narrowing my eyes at her.

All she did was smirk, avoiding eye contact with me. "I have my people."

I jabbed her in the side with my finger before gathering her in my arms unexpectedly and launching into the sky, laughing at her shocked chirp.

We flew over Ghita, waving at the townspeople who dared look up at us in the sky, the sun setting on the horizon. Cara relaxed in my arms, and I caught her admiring the view from above, so I flew just a little higher to see the expanse of the kingdom from the Black Avalanches to the edges of Mariande and Eldamain.

When we landed on our front lawn, I set her feet on the ground and let her get her bearings. She took a few steps back, her gaze bouncing from me to our house.

"Are you staying the night?" she asked, tilting her head.

I sighed, pressing my lips in a tight line. "I already know Voss isn't going to be happy I spent the whole day here. It was only supposed to be for a little bit. He and Ibis will probably be asleep by the time I get back."

"That's okay." She shrugged before slipping her arms around my waist, holding me close in a warm hug.

"I miss you every day," I whispered to her, pressing a kiss to the side of her head. "I can't wait for the day you can join me in the sky."

"I'm very proud of who you've become," she said, surprising me. I reclined my head to look at her, but she kept her cheek pressed to my shoulder. "But don't let them take away everything that makes you Remy."

I stared off toward the Black Avalanches, blinking away my shock at the statement because I wasn't sure what she meant by what made me Remy.

"When you love, you love so fiercely. It is like the stars lighting the night sky. Who knows what that love could do for a man like Ibis." She finally pulled her head back to meet my gaze, tears lining them. "Don't rob him of that love. Don't rob the world of that love."

Chapter 7

I woke the next morning with a few hours of sleep under my belt, rolling off my rock-hard mattress and onto the floor with a groan. My internal clock already told me it was still too early for Voss to be awake, but I heard the faint clanging of pots and pans in the kitchen as Ibis readied for breakfast.

I threw on a knit sweater to fight the morning chill, and I considered allowing Ibis his alone time in the kitchen, something he seemed to value since he made all our meals. But my conversation with Cara about not really knowing him and potentially being in love with him kept replaying in my head, so I went against my better judgment and emerged into the open living space.

Ibis held up hand in a half wave before resuming his preparation and organization. I shuffled across the stone floor to the island in the middle of the kitchen, leaning my elbows against the wooden surface.

"Could I help you cook?" I blurted before I realized what I was actually asking. Ibis was equally as caught off guard because he stilled in front of the stove, his back muscles clenched.

I was about to take it back and hide in the depths of my room when he looked over his shoulder with a raised eyebrow, then silently ushered me over with a jerk of his head.

My stomach fluttered as I carefully made my way around the

island, my heart thundering in my chest as I dramatically saddled up beside him, wiggling my shoulders. He rolled his eyes, but the ghost of the smirk that occasionally graced his lips peeked out.

"What do you know of a kitchen?" he inquired, his voice rumbling in the air as he spoke.

"Well, you know I'm good with the potions," I reminded him, holding my hands out over the stovetop flame he'd started. "I also grew up helping my mother cook, so I know how to be a very good assistant."

He was quiet at first as he placed a pan in front of me on top of the heat. He seemed to contemplate what to say before the corner of his lip twitched up. "Are you trying to tell me you're good at following directions?"

I glared at him from the corners of my eyes as he dropped two eggs in both of my outstretched hands. I bit my tongue at the retort I had about the enjoyment I found in being commanded.

"Get the eggs ready for us," Ibis ordered, not unkindly.

I bit my tongue harder as I cracked the eggs into the pan.

I cleared my throat before asking, "So why do you like to cook so much? I'm assuming it has something to do with it being one of the few moments you get alone time, especially since I've been around."

Those walls around Ibis were more than evident as he drew his face and shoulders tight, a muscle flexing in his jaw. Whether they had been built as a result of something in his past or under the direction of Voss and his belief to never love in order to get ahead, I wasn't sure, but I knew if I could just breach them once…

"It helps me clear my mind," he began quietly, throwing a mixture of vegetables into another pan and oats into a pot of boiling water. "Well, not clear my mind necessarily. It just helps me sort through thoughts and quiets my mind. It just depends on the day."

"I get that." I shrugged and cocked my head toward that empty firepit in the middle of the room. "I have the same thing with the potions—"

"It keeps me connected to my mother, too," he blurted, wincing at himself. He shook his head as he frowned at the pot. "She always let me experiment in the kitchen and taught me how to gauge flavor. Sometimes, if I close my eyes, she's still right next to me."

"My mother would *never*," I scoffed, smiling at the thought of my poor mother letting me experiment in the kitchen. "She always said I was only allowed in the kitchen if I followed her rules. Otherwise, the whole place would come down. And those were her exact words."

Ibis chuckled at that, the sound automatically bringing a smile to my face as he said, "Why am I not surprised? A chaotic adult must have meant an *utterly* chaotic child."

I snickered as I thought about my talk with Cara again. This was one of the most civil conversations Ibis and I'd had outside of training or education with Voss, but he wasn't shocked at something from my past because he *knew* me just as much as I knew him.

"Home is Riddling, right?" I flipped the eggs before turning my gaze on him. The fire underneath the pots lit up his golden eyes like a candle illuminating a glass of whiskey.

Something akin to sadness flashed in those deep hues—such a foreign emotion on his serious face—but it softened those hard edges and hit me in the chest.

"Yes, Riddling is home," he whispered, keeping his head lowered. "I haven't seen my family since I came here."

"Not once?" I frowned, trying to read him. There were so many emotions flashing across his face, I didn't know where to start: sadness, anger—to which I was accustomed—and potentially guilt.

"Do you miss them?"

"Of course I miss them," he snapped, just barely turning his head to me. "But this life we want to live is better off without attachments. Without something for a kingdom to hold against you to bargain—"

"I just don't understand," I interrupted, resting the spatula on the counter to face him. "Why would we want to work for kingdoms that are going to use our families against us?"

"Because working for kingdoms is the only way Magics can make it in this world," Voss called from the living area. I rolled my eyes, catching that small smile on Ibis's face as I twirled around to Voss.

"I have a hard time believing that," I argued, tilting my head to the side. "I come from a town that has plenty of successful establishments. The Great Karasi herself is ascribed to no kingdom, and from what I've learned, Jorah of Mariande doesn't work for the royal family."

Voss's gray eyes narrowed as he folded his arms across his chest and tilted his head. "Do you know how those two live? They still have to hide their existence, masking it with fronts. Karasi has a code you must utter to even find her home, while Jorah hides within the depths of that jewel store, behind his workers and a false owner."

"So, without recognition and safety?" I stepped around the island, just barely registering the soft caress of Ibis's fingers on the inside of my wrist. I kept walking though, wanting to push Voss's line of thinking. "You do realize Magics hide because they don't know how to defend themselves. If they knew how, having to be employed by kingdoms and secluding ourselves from those we love wouldn't be the only option to have a normal, secure existence."

"It would take too much to educate the masses on self-defense alone." Voss took careful steps toward me, scrutinizing me. "That does not include teaching them to bite back before a kingdom bites first. We don't know the true population of Magics in a given country, nor do we know how much their powers vary in strength, stamina, or other gifts they do not know how to tap into."

"That's the problem." I wagged my finger at him, my other hand perched on my hip. "It took me an hour to teach my sister to tap into her Magic well. After that, she was able to run as fast as me, throw a decent punch, considering she never has—not that I know of anyway—"

"But that is one Magic," Voss exclaimed, holding up one finger, "whose brother possesses rare qualities we do not find often. It is not surprising she has the same strength as you. But what of your neighbor? There are Magics who simply do not have the cleanest of blood because of their mortal ancestors or parents, therefore weakening their abilities."

My eyebrows pressed together as I took a step back, assessing Voss from the top of his braided head to the bottom of his boots. "*Clean* blood? Do you mean to tell me you're hypothesizing Magics have become diluted because we've bred with mortals? Because I *know* you can't possibly prove that."

Voss straightened, his nostrils flaring as he took a deep breath in. I chanced a glance behind me at Ibis, who was also looking at Voss with suspicion as if this was the first he'd heard Voss speak in that way.

When I looked back at our mentor, he had recovered, his hands now locked behind his back with his head inclined. "I mentioned once before, Remiel, that it is important to detach in order to be successful. The basis of this discussion is that you need to learn to let your family go."

I threw my shoulders back and almost told him where to stick the basis of this discussion when Ibis interrupted the almost-fight. "Breakfast is ready, Remiel."

The rarity of my name on his lips—in *that* voice—was enough to stop me in my tracks. I twirled around, locking eyes with the winged man on the other side of the island as I braced a hand on top. I vaguely heard the door shut behind me, and a brief glance back revealed Voss had left.

A hand slipped over mine, again preventing me from stalking after the old man. I stared at Ibis's hand, warm and comforting.

When I met his eyes again, his walls were back up, but there was something underneath them that felt special, like a crack in a door reserved only for me and those Ibis let in.

"You don't have to agree with him," Ibis whispered quietly, a conversation just between us. "I still don't think I agree with detaching from your family. I miss my parents every single day. When I left, I didn't know how to tell them why I was going, and things didn't end well between us. I don't know if I'll be able to ever see them again.

"But if your family is the reason you're here, and they support you no matter what decision you make..." Ibis shrugged, removing his hand from mine. "They'll be there when you're done here. Even if it's a temporary detachment. There are always ravens to send letters."

I was glued to his expression that wasn't a scowl for once. The longer I stared, the deeper the red in his cheeks got beneath his golden tone. He averted his gaze, mixing his food on his plate.

"Eat your food, Remiel."

Chapter 8

Summertide 1783 A.V.

2 Months Later

I sat beside Ibis on top of a plateau within the Black Avalanches, one that overlooked the northern side. The massive forest known as The Overgrowns crawled from Main Town—also known as the Forgotten City—to the very tip of the continent. I chuckled to myself at the thought of how much these two liked to perch on high places, considering the mythical animals they descended from were bird-like.

"Something funny, *nychterída?*" Ibis asked from where he sat on the ledge, his head tipped back.

"We're perched like *birds* again," I explained, waving my hand in the air above my head. "I find it funny that the House of Nemea likes to perch on places."

"Says the bat." Ibis sneered, but underneath that was a playful tone Ibis had taken on over the last few months.

A small smirk ticked at the corners of my lips as my stomach flipped. "Bats like to hang upside down in dark places, not *perch.*"

"I'd imagine you can't see many useful things upside down," Ibis challenged, an eyebrow raised.

"You'd be surprised the *things* you're closer to when you're upside down." I let my gaze flicker from his face to his lap and back again, that blush creeping onto his cheeks already. "Anatomically speaking—"

"Gentleman," Voss grumbled from where he sat, playing with the stupid rope he'd brought in case we were still up here by nightfall. "While I am glad the tension between you two has subsided over the last year, I would appreciate it even more if we kept the crudeness to a minimum, *Remiel*."

Little did he know the tension from my end never went away. As for Ibis, it seemed like the tension he was feeling had morphed into the more attractive nature I'd been experiencing since the moment we met.

In the aftermath of our moment in the kitchen, his inclusion of me extended beyond our typical tasks to meal prepping, which allowed us time alone throughout our days to talk about anything we wanted—or nothing at all. I'd also caught him watching me when I did anything without a shirt, which did nothing good for my ego.

But Voss's rule about attachment hung heavily between us, so I never dared push it.

I just recognized his admiration with a subtle, quick wink every single time.

"Now, I've heard you both talk about your home life and where you are from or where your families are from over the last few months," Voss began, studying us before locking his gaze on Ibis. "Have you told him exactly who you reign from?"

Ibis didn't even acknowledge Voss but rather stared off into the expanse of The Overgrowns.

"Do you mean his lineage, or is there some drama regarding who the real father is?" I asked, gauging Ibis's reaction.

I nearly dropped to the floor dead when the corner of his mouth quirked up, and he closed his eyes.

"Do you know of the demi-gods, Remiel?" Voss asked, tilting his head to the side.

"I'm assuming you mean for Magics." I nodded slowly, listing them on my fingers. "There is Sybil, who was the daughter of the Goddess Morana and a Magic. She is credited with designating the House of Echidna. Brigid, the daughter of the God Rod and a Magic, created the House of Argo, while Garuda, the son of Rod and a Magic, created the House of Nemea…"

I trailed off as I realized what Voss now meant by Ibis's descendancy. I slowly dragged my attention back to Ibis to find him still studying The Overgrowns as if his demi-god, many-times-great-grandfather would emerge from them.

"You're descended from Garuda?" I asked, trying to get a read on him from the side of his face. "You're the descendant of a demi-god and, therefore, a God?"

"Garuda was born nearly four thousand years ago," Ibis laughed, the sound settling in my bones and making my cock twitch. "Voss acts as though he were my grandfather. The inheritance is barely anything now. He could just as well be a descendant of Garuda as me, just as your entire House could be descendants of Sybil."

"I wouldn't go that far." I eyed him with a brow risen. "I don't even know if Sybil had children."

"When it comes to descendants of demi-gods, there are no family trees to directly trace our heritage," Voss explained, setting his rope to the side. "All we have are legends carried down through our families, generation after generation."

"That's the only way you know?" I asked, shifting on the ledge to face Ibis. "By word of mouth?"

"There is one other way to know your family descends from

demi-gods." Ibis twisted on the ground, massaging his thumb into his palm. "Back when demi-gods and their descendants roamed Aveesh, there was some concern that they would yearn for greater power and be driven mad by what power they did have. To keep them tethered to this world, Magics forged hematite pendants and jewelry. The hematite, imbued with Magic blood, has the ability to mute the powers of a demi-god descendant. It's like a leash."

"So, you have one of these pendants?" I only ever noticed the gold hoop earring and nose ring Ibis always wore. "Where is it?"

"It's in my room," Ibis admitted with a nod. "I never wear it because I find I can't bring forth my wings when wearing it, and my powers in general are harder to access. Almost as if it's thrashing, and I can't quite grasp it."

"Why hematite?" I directed my question to Voss then. "And why Magic blood? I never understood what about our blood made potions more effective either."

"It stems from how Magics came to be." Voss stood from where he had been sitting and began to pace as he spoke. "As we've discussed, the Goddess Morana planted the souls of mortals within the mythological creatures of Aveesh so the Gods could converse with them. In doing so, Magics were god-touched, which meant our blood was enhanced compared to the mortals, similar to the Sirians.

"Being god-touched is what gives us all of our enhanced abilities, and our connection to the creatures is what allows us to shift. Well, those who still can, anyway. By adding our blood to potions, those who take them are given what is essentially a god-touched potion, improving the efficacy of the mixture."

"I don't understand how Magic blood would help the hematite stone mute *Magic* abilities, then." I pursed my lips, trying to keep track of yet another history lesson I didn't ask for. "Wouldn't that sort of counteract whatever the hematite does naturally?"

"First of all, hematite does not mute Magic abilities," Voss clarified, pointing at me. "This is an important distinction. It only mutes the abilities of a demi-god, which means hematite will also mute the abilities of demi-god Sirians and their descendants."

"Okay," I drawled while glancing briefly at Ibis. I point my thumb at him. "So, if I don't descend from a demi-god, me wearing his pendant won't do anything to me?"

"If you don't reign from a demi-god, no." Voss resumed his pacing. "The hematite stone comes from the Black Avalanches. There is something innately *other* about the hematite stone that, according to legends, the Gods always despised. That is why our myths always connect the Black Avalanches to the Gods. Some believe it is how Kuk and Khonsa came to Aveesh from wherever they journeyed from, while others believe it is because they hated them due to the hematite stone deep within."

"So, imbuing it with Magic blood enhances its properties for Gods and demi-god descendants." I assumed that meant the Magic blood that coated or soaked the stone—whatever the process was—would have to be normal Magic blood and not demi-god descendant. Otherwise, that would neutralize the effectiveness and make this other power of the hematite stone null.

"Well, I guess we can always test whether I'm descended from a demi-god or not by putting the hematite pendant on me." I wiggled my eyebrows at Ibis but was shocked when he cocked his head to the side, those wheels in his mind turning. "Oh, Gods. We're doing it, aren't we?"

We all flew at top speed toward the cave to try and make it back before it was too dark, and we'd have to use the rope. We all raced inside one after the other like children on their birthdays, Voss and I waiting not-so-patiently in the living room as Ibis trudged to his room to collect his pendant.

"If I descend from a demi-god, would it be Sybil?" I asked, frowning as I gnawed at my lower lip.

"We may never know." Voss shrugged, tapping his foot. "Your mother reigns from Argo, does she not? You could descend from Brigid."

"Even if I inherited the Echidna traits?"

Ibis walked out with his hand clenched in a fist and Voss ushered him over as he answered, "It is still demi-god blood that runs in your veins, then."

I held my breath as Ibis produced a simple, circular black stone attached to a pin with gold wiring. He fixated on my chest as he carefully held my shirt in his hands, fastening the pendant to it. Once it was attached, he slowly blinked at me, just inches separating us.

"Your wings are still out," Ibis whispered as we got lost in each other's eyes, my purple to his gold. "Do you feel like your power is upset?"

I didn't feel any different, not when it came to my power, at least. All I could feel was the magnetic pull to Ibis, the urge to brush my fingers along his sharp jawline, to run my fingers through those tight, brown curls.

I swallowed. "I don't feel anything."

I swore I saw relief in his face at my answer.

I heard Voss sigh in disappointment beside us as he stalked off toward his room, leaving Ibis and me in the middle of the living room.

Chapter 9

Autumnus 1783 A.V.

4 Months Later

For the first time since our relationship started to shift, Ibis and I were left alone for nearly twenty-four hours with a short chore list and no other instructions, which had me pondering what we could do for the entire day.

So, when I burst from my room, enthusiastically proclaiming that we were journeying into the Forgotten City of Eldamain, I almost doubled over laughing when Ibis startled on the couch, clutching his chest.

"Main Town?" Ibis gawked at me as if I had a second head growing on my shoulders. "Are you out of your mind?"

"Most of the time, yes," I said, plopping down beside him on the couch. "Come on. When was the last time you felt joy, bird boy?" He shot me a sidelong glare. "The only rule we were given when Voss left was to get the chores done, which we already did. Main Town is not even a thirty-minute flight from here. We could go there for the afternoon and make it back before sundown. Even if we don't, we bring a rope so I can get you back here."

"Remiel," Ibis drawled in warning, shaking his head. "Are you sure you're willing to test Voss again? You've been pushing your limits with him lately."

"He's not coming back until the morning," I exclaimed,

gripping his forearm. I tugged on his arm, nearly begging. "Please, Ibis? I've been good for the last year and a half, and I'm dying to have a little fun. We're young, right? You're—what—like twenty-five?"

Ibis deadpanned, his left eye twitching. "I'm only twenty-one, *nychterída*."

"Oh, shit," I laughed, throwing my head back. "You're always so fucking serious. I didn't realize we're only two years apart."

He couldn't stay serious after that as the most radiant smile climbed up his lips. "I am not serious all the time."

It was my turn to stare at him through heavy-lidded eyes. "Ibis… Live a little, will ya?"

That must have sparked something in him because his eyes reflected his smile, and he lurched from the couch, his wings springing from his back. My heart fluttered in my chest as I followed suit, enjoying the foreign, devious little glint in Ibis's eye as he winked at me and flew out the door.

·⋆☆⋅☽⋅✯⋆·

Shockingly, I'd never been to Main Town before. I lived a majority of my life within Ghita's boundaries in The Clips, despite Eldamain being a place for Magics.

Since the fall of their kingdom nearly one thousand years ago, Eldamain was considered a sort of outsider or no-man's land. A territory owned by The Clips, Magics flocked here for centuries to seek asylum. While they were not safe from their fair share of assaults and harassments, it was less likely those who tend to be the most aggressive from Etherea and Teslin would venture as far north as Eldamain to pick on Magics.

Even Mariande kept their distance from the Magics gathered here.

Home to the Great Karasi, people only traveled to Eldamain in search of Magics when they needed them for something: a prophecy, a special potion, exclusive drugs, alcohol, or to satisfy a fantasy.

Main Town was the biggest Magic hub in the entire country, built on top of the ruins of a once-thriving city whose name no one remembered anymore. Magics lived scattered across Eldamain in an effort to remain secretive since that's the only way Magics can be safe, apparently.

Ibis and I walked through the ramshackle town, walking with trepidation up and down the sidewalks. Every building looked like it was *literally* built upon the stone ruins of the city that once thrived. While the bases of the structures were made of stone, roughly halfway up their walls it morphed into wooden panels with chipped paint that revealed different colors or raw wood underneath. Occasionally, we passed a marble or granite pillar, some empty of whatever monument once stood there, while others had jagged pieces of a figurine chopped at the shins or ankles.

"Is this how all the Magic communities are on the Main Continent?" Ibis asked, his eyes lingering on some secretive deal happening in an alleyway. Aside from a couple of people huddled mysteriously together, swapping items, there weren't many stores or restaurants to pop into. We walked by a handful of buildings that passed as pubs.

"Not at all." Multiple families scurried past one another with their gazes down. Even as the children's stares lingered on each other, the mothers and fathers just tugged them along. "Ghita is extremely close-knit. It's like what you would expect of any normal village. Children playing, people eating together, music in the streets—"

"That's how Chisisi is," Ibis exclaimed under his breath, splaying his hands out in front of him. "We celebrate the holidays as an entire village, we lean on each other for support, we share the wealth of the community… This is like…"

As he trailed off, I could only think of one way to describe what we saw. "I think what we come from are villages. Maybe this town doesn't have a name because it's not a town at all. It's just a main place where you can get what you need and go back home to your small circle. If they even have that."

"That's such a sad way of life," Ibis said, but I snapped my head to him in surprise.

I grabbed his hand, halting him mid-stride, his unnaturally smooth palm warm in mine. "Do you realize what you've just said?"

Ibis's eyebrow twitched, but he was so distracted by the startling difference between Main Town and where he came from—Chisisi, he called it—that he didn't realize how much this foreshadowed the life Voss wanted for both of us and himself.

"Let's grab some ale from one of these shops and head back to our perch." I held onto his hand as I dragged him to the closest merchant. "It's just the two of us regardless of where we are, it seems."

We slipped into a tiny storefront, and I grabbed the first pint of spirits I laid my eyes on. Ibis hung back by the front door as I exchanged coins with the man at the register, who was eyeing Ibis with suspicion.

"Is there a problem?" I inquired, tilting my head at the man. "I know he's pretty, but it's not polite to stare."

Ibis bristled behind me as the man flared his nostrils, squinting.

"I ain't seen wings from Nemea before," the man explained, gnawing on some green plant in his mouth. He cocked his head in the direction of Ibis. "I've been told he can fetch a pretty price on the market. A feather from them pretty wings can restore sight to the blind, a tear can bring you back from Morana's door." He looked at Ibis when he added, "You got claws, boy? I heard they can speed up healing."

"He doesn't, unfortunately," I sneered, snatching the brown bag from the cashier's hand. I held up my own that wasn't clutching the spirit, my claws shooting out. "But I do. Would you like to find out if my fangs are poisonous?"

"Remiel," Ibis called from the front door. I glanced over my shoulder, locking onto those eyes. Calm settled over me as he jerked his head toward the door. "Let's just go."

I faked a lunge at the man, which had him staggering back against the wall of liquor behind him. I blew him a kiss before heading for the door, grabbing Ibis's hand in mine again, and flying into the sky.

·⁺˚⋆☽⋆˚⁺·

We hung out on the same plateau we had last month, overlooking The Overgrowns and Main Town.

There was nothing left of the glorious city from a millennium ago, whatever it may have looked like in its prime.

"What were you getting at before we left?" Ibis asked, throwing back the whiskey we'd grabbed from the shop.

Go fucking figure that's what I grabbed.

I took it from him and drew back a gulp myself, nearly groaning at the burning familiarity that slithered down my throat. "You said the life they lived in Eldamain was sad, but that's the exact life Voss preaches to us. Isolation, seclusion… If it's so sad, why do you agree with him?"

Ibis didn't look at me as he blindly held out his hand for the liquor. I slid it into his grasp, my fingers tingling from where they brushed his.

"I wouldn't say I agree with him," Ibis said before throwing back another sip and wincing. "I will say that whole mention of the *clean* blood startled me. I think he's really focused on why some of us have the level of abilities and gifts we do, and that was one of his hypotheses, even if it's not the best choice of words.

"But I would also have to say I half agree with him," Ibis continued, handing me the bottle again. "While I do think the best position for a Magic is to use their abilities to have an in with a kingdom, I don't think we need to shun ourselves from the world. I think we can still have families and friends."

I studied him over the neck of the bottle as I slowly took a drink, never removing my eyes from him.

He shifted uncomfortably under my gaze, frowning. "What?"

"What is the *best position*?" I asked, mocking his low voice. He raised an amused eyebrow, suppressing his smile. "By your definition. What does that entail?"

"I mean, to be at the beck and call of a kingdom would mean to have high pay and status," Ibis explained, listing on his fingers. "You would have safety, freedom, jobs... Look at Voss. He's essentially retired, but he still gets called to kingdoms to do whatever it is they need him for. He's traveled all the continents under the protection of them—"

"Has he?" I inquired, leaning back on one hand as I balanced the bottle on my thigh. "Does he have knights protecting his back when he ventures to these kingdoms?"

"Well, no," Ibis drawled, squinting out toward the horizon. "He knows how to protect himself."

"So, his Magic abilities, that he knows how to use, protect him," I concluded, nodding slowly. "And when you say he's essentially retired, do you think *still* being at the beck and call of a country—even when you live in a cave—is freedom?"

"I mean, I did say essentially—"

"And what of your parents?" I waved the bottle toward him, then swung it behind me in the direction I assumed Riddling was. "Were they unhappy with their lives? What about those who lived in your village? Did they seem unhappy with their positions?"

"I grew up in a very happy home and village." Ibis frowned, clearly unsure of where I was going still.

I wagged my head side to side as I said, "And you're alive, so wouldn't you say you were safe where you lived?"

The fervor with which Ibis spoke about this *best position* slowly faded from his eyes as he understood what I was saying.

"Voss's way is not the end all be all," I began, handing him the bottle. I chuckled as he took a long swig. "I can empathize with you if you want a high-paying, high-ranking position somewhere within a kingdom. That's all you, then. But if you are doing it because you want freedom, safety, and just to live, it is not the only way to do so. My parents made a great living making potions. A village has a plethora of ways to collect an income.

"Do you know why I stay, Ibis?" I stared in the direction of Main Town, where the people cowered from one another, their own kind. "I want to learn all I can from Voss about fighting and protection and accessing your Magic well. When he realizes I don't want the future he's drilled into you, I know he's going to kick me out as his apprentice. But I don't care."

"Why?" Ibis scoffed, curling a lip. "Why can't you be roused to care about anything other than yourself?"

I whirled my head on him, my chest tightening. "I could say the same about you, bird boy."

He startled, leaning away from me as he clutched the bottle to his chest.

"There are thousands of Magics out there," I whispered, flinging my arms out. "I know you were taught to fight in Riddling, but we don't even know how to tap into our wells on the Main Continent. Magics just try to get by and exist, establishing little communities where they can until a kingdom comes and runs them out. If not, you go to Eldamain and just try to live your life in peace.

"But hiding out in a cave, learning all these incredible skills, just to go work for the exact kingdoms that would rather see us wiped off Aveesh?" I shook my head as Ibis slowly sat upright again. "That's selfish. We could save hundreds of Magics if we taught them what Voss teaches us. They'd be able to defend their towns. Hell, we could even rise up and demand respect if we could teach multiple villages across the continent."

"You want to teach Magics?" Ibis's eyes scanned my face incessantly as he placed the bottle between us on the stone ground.

"Imagine," I paused, breathless, "if the entire country of Eldamain learned how to fight, to protect themselves… They could rise up. They could claim the country as theirs—as *ours*—and put Magics on a throne that's been empty for a thousand years. We'd have our own country."

My chest rose and fell with excited breaths, and I didn't realize how fast my heart rate had picked up during my speech. A strange sort of energy spread through me at the thought of my plan to help succeeding, at the real freedom and safety Magics would have if it all worked out.

I hadn't realized I'd been smiling until a hand brushed my arm, causing the smile to falter. I glanced down at Ibis's tanned hand, which contrasted with my paler skin, the warmth from it spreading up my arm. I steadily dragged my gaze up to meet his, and his face softened entirely.

It was like looking upon a God, like looking upon the sun itself, that tenderness he regarded me with blooming in my chest.

"You beautiful dreamer," Ibis whispered, his thumb stroking over the top of my hand.

I looked back down at where our hands joined, gripping his fingers in between mine. I peered at him through my lashes as I gently pulled him closer, my heart pounding against my ribcage as he let me. The distance between us decreased with each breath, time ceasing around us.

With our foreheads nearly touching, his eyes fluttered as I brushed his nose with mine. I trailed my hand up his arm to grip the side of his neck and ran my thumb across his chin and sharp jawline.

"Remiel," Ibis breathed, the air between us mingling. "I don't know if…"

He didn't need to finish that sentence because I already knew what he was going to say. As long as we were Voss's apprentices, we couldn't cross that line. He also didn't know, but I was already in love with him, and I wasn't sure what it would do to me if we made things physical.

Especially if he still wanted to follow Voss's lead when it came to his future.

"You're right," I sighed, letting my hand drop back to my side as we slowly separated.

But there was a new twinkle in those gleaming eyes as he let them travel across my face from my own eyes to my lips and around my head.

"Besides," Ibis grunted as he stood to full height and stood on the edge of the plateau, his back facing the cliffside, "I don't kiss on the first date."

With that, Ibis free-fell backward, and I jumped upright just as he shot back up into the sky, disappearing within the clouds of the mountain's peaks. A smile spread across my face as he hollered somewhere above me, calling my name.

I shot up into the sky, zooming past Ibis, who was nearly invisible, the white of his wings blending with the clouds. I looked down at him from where I flapped my wings, marveling at the sunset streaming through the cracks of the puffy white and hitting Ibis like a glowing beacon in the sky.

"Don't you remember, Remiel?" Ibis called from below, grinning ear-to-ear. "It's not polite to stare."

I gaped when he fell under a layer of clouds, shouting some nonsense about me being the pretty boy. As I followed him through the sky, I threw my head back and laughed into the winds.

Chapter 10

Springtide 1784 A.V.

5 Months Later

I hunched over the fire in the middle of the cave, boiling the oil filled with various herbs and trying to control the level of heat applied to the pot. Every so often, a breeze would funnel down the hole in the ceiling, and the flames would flare around the pot, nearly dipping into its contents over the rim.

The front door suddenly jerked open, and Ibis stumbled inside carrying a rolled piece of parchment that had arguably seen better days. Voss scurried in from down the hall, his wings tucked in protectively. When he realized it was Ibis, the tension left his shoulders, but he cocked his head to the side.

"What do you have there, boy?" Voss frowned, pointing in the direction of the parchment gripped in Ibis's fist.

But Ibis wasn't looking at Voss. He stared at me, his eyes downturned and a slight frown on his face. He took hesitant steps, rolling his lips together as he carefully extended the parchment between us.

My eyes bounced from the parchment to Ibis's dim golden eyes, my stomach hollowing out. "What is it?"

"I think it'd be best if you read it," Ibis softly said, urging me to accept the parchment.

I shook my head violently, pushing out my bottom lip. "No. I can see you read it. What is it?"

"I can't—" Ibis cut himself off by snapping his mouth shut. He exhaled harshly through his nose, staring down at the piece of paper in his hand before dragging his piercing gaze back to me. "Please, Remiel. Don't make me be the one to deliver this."

"I *need* you to be the one that delivers this," I whispered back, still unsure of what it was we spoke of, but I knew it wasn't good. Maybe, in a way, I always knew a letter that invoked this much pity from someone who usually hid behind a brick wall was never good.

"It's Ghita." Ibis swallowed, his hand gradually finding its way back to his side, clutching the note. "It was attacked."

I saw nothing and everything at once as my vision tunneled, my heart ceasing to beat in my chest. Without a second thought, I marched off down the hallway toward my room, swinging my door open and grabbing a cap and scarf. My blood rushed in my ears and the sound of my pulse drowned out Ibis and Voss's arguing, their voices distant and muffled.

"Let him," I heard one of them say, almost like a plea.

"He must get used to loss." The voice was low enough to be a growl. "Working for royal kingdoms means no attachments. *You would do best to remember that, boy.*"

I charged into the living room to find Ibis and Voss huddled over the island. Their heads snapped to me, and while Voss stood his ground with arms crossed, Ibis closed the short distance between us. He grabbed my shoulders to force me to look at him.

"Remiel," Ibis whispered, his eyes scanning my face.

"You will not leave, *drakon*," Voss warned, narrowing his eyes. "No matter what may wait for you in Ghita, you must let it go. Attachments are only a weakness if you are to work with any kingdom. It is safer for any family you may have if you leave them behind. It does not do well to dwell on the things we've left behind."

"I need to know if they're okay," I snapped, lurching toward Voss, but Ibis tightened his hands on my shoulders to hold me back. I didn't think I'd fight Voss, but my strength was intensifying and buzzing under my skin.

"Think about this before you go," Ibis pleaded, his eyes wild. "This apprenticeship is meant to prepare us for the future—for *our* futures…"

Voss took an impending step forward, his hands clasped behind his back. "We are not meant to carry these things with us. I am more than one-hundred-and-fifty, and it is highly possible I still have a least one-hundred years ahead of me. Considering you are showing to be more powerful than I, you are more than likely to outlive your family—"

"You don't know that!" I snarled, trying to shake off his grip. "My sister is still young. She could show gifts, too, and if she's alone, I have to go help her. If she's…"

I trailed off because I didn't dare utter the words aloud. Ibis caught what I was going to say, and the sadness in his eyes deepened as he took my face in his hands, startling me.

"I have led you these last two years, molded you into the Magic and the man you are today." Voss unfolded his arms with his wings flaring out on either side of him. "You have only gotten to this point by doing what you're told, so you will do as I say now. I warned you this moment would come when you would need to detach from your family, and this is the time. Whether they be alive or dead, this is the opportunity to let them go."

"What is wrong with you?" I whispered, staring in disbelief as I tipped my head back. My voice gradually rose as I continued, "A town was *attacked*. There could be survivors beyond just my family.

How can you do nothing when your own people die around you?"

"Why do you think it is our responsibility to save our species?" Voss took another step forward, and my power thrummed in my veins. Ibis tried to keep me from looking at Voss by pivoting himself in front of me. "Ghita is one town and Magics are spread across our world in various states of hiding. We cannot protect every single town with simply three of us when we have an entire country full of Magics at our backs, cowering in the shade of a mountain at the northernmost tip of a continent."

I flinched, curling my lip back. Even Ibis stiffened in front of me, a slight twitch to his eyebrows. I stepped into Ibis, calling out over his shoulder, "This is what I've been talking about, Voss. We could change that. We have to change that."

"You want to be a hero, boy?" Voss marched forward, closing the distance so Ibis was essentially trapped between us. "To be a hero, you have to sacrifice what you love. But you won't sacrifice *your* mortal attachments."

"Says the man who collects bones on a wall," I snarled, jerking in Ibis's grip.

Voss jutted out his chin in a sneer and crossed his arms. "How can you be a hero when you aren't willing to sacrifice what you love?"

My shoulders slumped and Ibis's grip loosened on them. I dragged my gaze to those beautiful, whiskey eyes that drowned me the moment I met him. I ate in every detail of his face, committing it to memory because I knew what I was about to do, as one of the last things Cara said to me before I left echoed in my mind.

Who said I wasn't going to sacrifice what I loved?

"Don't leave," Ibis begged and his voice cracked in the low whisper only meant for us.

I cupped his cheek in my hand, reveling in the scratch of his stubble against my palm. I brushed the tip of my nose against his and whispered, "Find me."

With that final pledge, I twisted out of his arms and flew out the front door toward the family that taught me what it meant to love.

I dropped into Ghita, and as I rose from my crouch, I noticed the town was eerily quiet. I tuned into my surroundings, listening for signs of life and people running about, but there was nothing.

Not even an animal scurried around as if they too had been killed in whatever carnage occurred.

For a moment, I thought maybe there was a mistake because the street was empty, save for overturned carts and scattered vegetables and trinkets. I followed the trail of destroyed corner shops, my eyes catching the blood smeared along stone walls and down walkways.

The closer I got to the town square, the stronger the scent of iron became as I noticed more and more deep maroon marks on every building and side street. The heels of my boots clicking echoed around me like a clock counting down.

As I stumbled out of an alleyway, a reveal it was.

I gagged, nearly emptying the contents of my stomach as I hooked my elbow over my nose and mouth to breathe in the scent of my clothes rather than the smell of murder that assaulted me.

Bodies were scattered haphazardly around the fountain in the middle of the open courtyard that glistened red. I could barely tell where one body started and one ended since some were piled on top of one another, either as a last effort to protect the person beside them or because they'd been thrown that way.

I carefully stepped around the bodies, from the elderly to the children, my eyes watering and skin tightening over my bones. My heart throbbed in the pit of my stomach, my chest tight as I fought the urge to run from this place.

But I needed to know if they were here. I had to find them.

I wasn't sure how long I had surveyed the entire mass grave site that was Ghita's main circle of business. A quick glance down various alleyways and sidewalks told me they all mimicked the one I'd traversed down.

They had corralled the Magics of Ghita like cattle, trapping them within the square without a single exit available to them, and slaughtered them where they huddled in fear.

It came to me then: the men I'd seen signaling up and down the streets, Cara saying Etherean knights had been in town…

My anger flared, my muscles tensing and my veins pulsing with my power. My vision tunneled further as I completed my search.

If they weren't here, the last place they would have been was at home.

I leaped into the sky and made a beeline for my home. The tree in the yard grew nearer and nearer, as did the Black Avalanches looming on the horizon, taunting me with the future I left behind…

My sun.

I landed directly between the house and the tree, crouching on the ground with my hand braced between my legs. I closed my eyes and just *listened*.

The silence here felt heavier, as though someone had draped a tent over our plot. It pulsed menacingly, humming against my eardrums. I hesitated before reaching down to enhance my smell, still reeling from the stench of the massacre in Ghita.

When I inhaled, the bitterness in my mouth amplified, and the vomit wracked my body as I fell to my hands and knees. Anything I'd consumed that day came out in a torrent that had me choking and gasping for air. After it relented, tears ran down my face, and I tried to take another deep breath.

I instantly regretted it as the horrid smell infiltrated every part of me, clinging to my nostrils and planting itself in my mind. I exhaled a mix between a cough and a sob because there was no way what awaited me in my home was anything better than what I'd witnessed in town.

I stood at the threshold, gawking at the door, which was precariously hanging on a single hinge, the bottom splintered in one of the corners. I swallowed against the burning in my throat, prayed up to the heavens, and stepped into my home one last time.

I nearly fell to my knees at the sight of my mother and father in the kitchen. My breath immediately became trapped in my lungs.

My father's eyes were still open with a glassy film over them. His deep blue hues that had shone with pride the last time I saw him were now staring into the endless void. Dried blood clung to the corner of his mouth, smeared across his cheek where it looked to have clumped in his beard.

Taking a few cautious steps further into the home, I stumbled into the table as I caught the edge and found my mother—Gods, my *incredible* mother—curled up beside my father with that same empty stare. Her white hair was covered in patches of blood, soaked at the ends where it dipped into the deep red pool surrounding them like an aura.

My father had a single wound straight to his heart, while my mother looked to have multiple wounds scattered about her torso, and a gash lashed across her cheek.

I whimpered as I stumbled towards the hallway, my vision blurring and tilting as my blood thrummed in my ears. My own quick, uneven breaths in my head echoed as I braced either hand on the walls beside me for balance, forcing myself forward. I dragged my feet behind me across our stained wooden floor, where bloodied footprints led me to Cara's bedroom.

The stench intensified as I neared her room, and my stomach churned again at the thought of what I would find. I squeezed my eyes shut, whispering, "Please, Gods, no. Please, not her."

I curled my body around the doorframe, peering into her room.

The scream that ripped from my throat scratched it raw before it tapered into a silent sob that deflated my lungs. I nearly fainted from lack of oxygen as I teetered into the doorframe, the wood digging into my spine between my wings.

I inhaled a rattling breath only for another sob to shatter my soul as my body concaved in on itself, and I wrapped my arms around my midsection to keep myself together.

Laying on the bed, completely naked, was my baby sister. The only reason I knew it was her was because of those wild, brown locks, identical to my own, fanned around her in matted clumps. Otherwise, she was nearly unrecognizable from the abuse her body sustained.

Her face was bruised and puffed, the eye sockets swollen shut and her nose twisted at a grotesque angle. Her body was littered with gashes and slices of varying degrees, her normal pink sheets now dyed maroon from her blood soaking into them.

The longer I stared at Cara… I could hear her screams embedded into the walls, the floor, the very foundation of this home. I clamped my hands over my head as I slid down the wall and pulled my legs into me. I cried into my knees, my shoulders shaking violently.

Memories flashed in my mind of Cara and my parents, from my earliest memories of holding her the day she was born to laughing with my mother in the kitchen. Their faces popped into my head, but they slowly morphed into the state in which they all rested now.

I replayed my last encounter with Cara over and over in my head, thinking about her beautiful smile and the pure wonder on her face as she beheld the world from above, stretching out across the horizon.

I can't wait for the day you can join me in the sky.

Everything around me fell away when I realized that Cara would never fly: the never-ending silence, the smell of Cara's decaying body, the ache in my wings from the angle I sat—all of it, gone. My cries subsided as a bone-deep ache crept in, settling along every joint and tendon. I slowly lifted my head, letting it lull back against the doorframe as my breathing settled and the tears dried against my cheeks.

A familiar darkness snuck into the corners of my mind, advancing on me like flies on the corpses strewn about my childhood home. It wrapped around my shoulders like a heavy, wool blanket, itching at the exposed parts of my skin. It sunk its claws into my mind, filing every feeling into a deep abyss to be forgotten.

I let the isolation descend.

My face went slack as I rose from the ground, avoiding the bodies that would remind me of the pain shooting through my chest and piercing my heart. I marched out the door and stood on the porch, relishing in the cleaner air, even if the sting of blood still clung to me.

I couldn't go back in there—wouldn't go back in there.

With a raw throat and dry mouth, I groaned against the roughness as I launched into the sky and headed southwest.

I needed a drink.

Chapter 11

Early Springtide 1785 A.V.

Nearly One Year Later

I leaned into the beautiful man beside me, looking up at him through bated lashes as he lit my cigar. I puffed the smoke up between us, and his dark hues flashed as the dealer called for our attention.

I settled into the red velvet chair, waving the cigar over the table as I nodded to the dealer.

He handed out the cards to each of the players, throwing my first perfectly in front of me. The nine of spades now sat precariously before me.

I took a drag from the cigar to keep me steady as the second card made its rounds. The queen of hearts winked at me as it settled beside the nine. My heart fluttered as the players to my right read their totals out loud, and my stomach twirled when it was my turn.

"Nineteen," I mumbled around the cigar.

I eyed the dealer's face card—the five of spades—as the guy to my left chirped his number. I wagged my head back and forth at the chances the Hole would force the dealer to draw again.

When the dealer silently raised an eyebrow to each player, some beckoned for another card with their finger or a tap on the table.

Again, the dealer came to me, and I pulled the cigar out of my mouth. "Stay."

When the final player between the dealer and I also stayed, silence descended over the table as we waited for the dealer to flip his card. In addition to the five of spades, he revealed the jack of clubs glistening in the lantern on the wall beside us, putting him at fifteen.

I toyed with the cigar between my fingers as my fellow players bristled beside me, waiting to see if they would be over, under, or if the dealer would bust.

I sat in horror as the dealer's third card winked at me.

The fucking five of diamonds, making his hand twenty.

The winning hand.

I shoved my chair out as I took a long drag of my cigar, walking to the bar without a tip.

I heavily slid into the leather stool as the bartender sidled up in front of me, leaning an elbow against the sleek, mahogany surface while buffing a champagne flute.

"What'll it be?" he asked, gnawing on a green plant, his eyes droopy.

"Make it a double." I placed my cigar in the tray before me as a flash of fire-red curls caught the corner of my eye. "And put it on his tab."

"You sit at that table for hours and don't even leave a Godsdamn tip, Remy," Hugo chuckled as he leaned on the bartop beside me, his sleeves rolled up to reveal thick, turquoise-scaled forearms. "And now you put your drink on *my* tab?"

"You know I'll be good for it." The bartender slid the amber liquid toward me as I side-eyed Hugo. "I'm your bounty hunter and your healer. Not much more I can do to pay off the debts."

"Maybe if you stopped drinking and gambling at the Obsidian

Coin during your free time, you'd have some cash to spare." Hugo dropped into the stool beside me, running a hand through his long, wild, red hair. "Really, it's the gambling, Remy. You have awful fucking luck."

"Oh, gee." I flashed him a dazzling grin, squinting. "Thanks, friend. Don't remind me."

Hugo beckoned the bartender with two light-toned fingers before tapping them on the bartop. "I don't know in what world you would consider us friends, Remy."

"I only let those I consider a friend call me Remy." I winked, tossing back the burning liquid with a slight wince.

He chuckled under his breath, staring at something on the shelf over the bartender's shoulder. "What would you have me call you instead?"

Nychterída jumped into my head unprovoked, along with a set of whiskey eyes that matched the amber liquid in Hugo's glass.

My chest clenched, and I swallowed against the lump in my throat, shaking my head. "Remiel is my formal title."

"Well, *Remy*," Hugo sneered, curling a somewhat unfriendly lip at me, his glass poised on his bottom lip, "take my advice. Cut back on the gambling. The drinking I couldn't give two shits about since I upcharge patrons for it. It's not like it's an expensive commodity."

"But I can't keep up with the gambling tab you're running." He tipped back the double shot in one hefty gulp, not a single muscle twitching. "And neither can you, so don't go pissing your earnings off on literally nothing. You're worth more than that."

"I'll keep that in mind," I grumbled under my breath, taking a final drag from my cigar. Hugo studied me from the corner of his eye with a strange look on his face, but I ignored it as I saluted him before stalking toward the man who'd lit my cigar.

I rolled my head on my neck, shutting my eyes against that statement. I wasn't worth shit, not anymore, but I wasn't about to wallow at the feet of a Magic kingpin. Like he said, we weren't friends. For the last year or so, he'd been my employer.

It seemed like my wings, fighting skills, and knack for potions came in handy not just for royal kingdoms but also for shady businesses in the heart of Teslin.

I'd stumbled into the Obsidian Coin after discovering my dead family, only to immediately dig myself into a hole, ready to let whatever henchmen the owner had beat me to a bloody pulp and throw me into the Red River.

Unfortunately, that owner happened to be Hugo, who was a measly year younger than me. He not only owned the Obsidian Coin but nearly a third of the various establishments in Rian and a Magic drug cartel.

Someone with that much money and power, and as many enemies as he did needed someone who could get business done quickly and cleanly and someone to help heal his own workers when they got into trouble.

The man from earlier lounged in one of the velvet couches beside a rack of brown and ruby red vials, observing me as I sauntered across the black marble floor, my boots clicking despite the relative level of chatter. I tilted my head to the side, raising an eyebrow at the female straddling his lap and grinding against his groin.

"Am I interrupting?" I asked, the side of my mouth twitching, no doubt revealing the sharp canine to the female. Her eyes connected with mine, the brick red irises startling.

"Just enjoying a dance." The male smiled, gesturing to the empty spot on the couch beside him. "Care to join me?"

I nodded once, keeping my attention latched onto the woman.

She was petite, not much to her, but those eyes were slightly unnerving. As I sunk into the plush cushion, she expertly twisted on her knee to straddle my lap, sashaying her hips so her pelvis brushed against my body.

"So, you're attracted to the—" I paused, studying her further. Pitch-black hair swished with every movement, sitting just above her shoulders. "The unique Magics."

"What makes you say that?" he asked, throwing his arm over the back of the couch. His hand hung just above my shoulder, not quite touching.

"Her eyes and rare features." I slipped my hand to the back of her head, gripping her hair and using it to angle her head towards him. She gasped quietly but didn't stop her dancing. "It's not often you get Magics like her from the Northern Pizi leaving their homeland."

I released my grip on her hair and relaxed further into the back of the cushion. I gripped her exposed thigh in my hand and slid my hand up her smooth skin, but I saw something dark and sad flash in her eyes. I smirked.

Just a dancer and one that had no interest in men.

"Then there's me." I winked at the man, chuckling at the blush that rose to his cheeks. "Purple eyes, fangs… And I bet you didn't know, but I have wings, too."

His eyebrows shot up, and I swore I could *smell* his arousal, which was definitely a new trick.

Unless I really just turned on this man that much.

"You don't say?" he mused, slowly turning his attention to the gathering patrons at the nearest table. "Echidna or Nemea?"

I articulated every word, staring into the side of his head. "Big. Black. Wings."

The man shifted in the seat, adjusting his pants as he averted his gaze.

"Dahlia," he said, putting a name to the small dancer in my lap. "Fetch one of your entertainers for me, would you?"

"Just one?" she asked, stepping back and fixing the barely-there lingerie she wore as a uniform.

The male painstakingly twirled his head, lolling it to the side as he assessed me with narrowed eyes. "A fun one."

⋆⋆☽⋆⋆

I kneeled at the foot of the bed and dragged my tongue up the center of the beautiful woman before me, digging my fingers into her supple thighs. She bucked her hips, throwing her head back against the pillows as a breathy moan trembled from her lips. I smirked before I went to work and curled my tongue inside her slick warmth, dragging it back out along her inner walls.

The man I'd linked up with at the Obsidian Coin straddled me from behind with his legs on either side of mine, lining himself up with my entrance. Anticipation coiled in my stomach as I felt his slick tip prod me, teasing.

Inch by inch, he slid himself within me, taking his sweet ass time. I momentarily threw my head over my shoulder, hissing, "Deeper."

He smirked at me before seating himself fully, hitting that spot that made my eyes roll to the back of my head. As he set his pace, I returned to the woman on the bed and pumped my fingers into her silky heat, making sure I gave a slight crook to them.

The man behind me continued to roll his hips, his member filling me, shocks of desire shooting through my body. I shut my eyes, groaning at the same time as the woman on the bed.

Just as he hooked his arm around my hips and grabbed my dick in his hand, the door to the room swung open and bounced off the wall.

"What the fu—" I lifted my head at the same time the man stopped slamming into me. The woman arched her back to get a look at the intruder standing in the doorway.

Nothing could've prepared me for who I saw taking up the entire frame, and for a moment, I thought maybe some of the mushrooms I'd consumed had been too potent, and I was hallucinating.

I withdrew my fingers from the woman, but I didn't want to leave her unsatisfied, so I coated my fingers with her cum and circled her clit. I tilted my head to the side, my gaze locked onto burning, whiskey eyes.

I faltered in my rhythm at the rage I saw burning in those eyes, my heart clenching at the sight of him. I thought of the last moment we saw each other a year ago and how he begged me to stay with him.

"Ibis," I chuckled, swallowing the lump in my throat. "What a *pleasure* it is to have you! Have you come to join us? We can most definitely accommodate you—"

"What in the Gods' names are you doing, Remiel?" Ibis ground out through clenched teeth, his fists curled up at his sides. He met the gazes of the man still seated inside me and the woman writhing on the bed and, in a menacing but erotic tone, demanded, "Out. Now."

The male behind me quickly withdrew and scurried around Ibis's intimidating figure standing within the room, just to the side of the door. The woman gathered her clothes and the man's, scrambling to get out just in time for Ibis to slam the door shut behind them.

Still kneeling by the bed, I gazed up at him from the other side, my smile spread ear-to-ear. "I knew you would want me all to yourself. You seem like a relationship type of guy—"

"Put your clothes on," Ibis snapped, averting his gaze. I glanced down at my body with my arms outstretched, my erection at full attention.

"You can't just stand there glistening with your *bulging* muscles and expect me to easily get rid of this through sheer will," I scoffed, motioning to my hard dick. He kept his eyes glued to the wall beside him, his nostrils flaring. "You can smell it, can't you—"

"You're a filthy Magic," Ibis sneered, his curled lip revealing that sharpened canine I just wish he'd sink into...

Well, anywhere.

With a heavy sigh, I relented, slipping on my slacks that were discarded nearby. I stood to my full height, rolling out my shoulders as I drank him in. His gaze jumped from my face down to my erection concealed in my pants and held there momentarily. His pupils dilated before he met my gaze again.

I raised an eyebrow, pursing my lips.

"What are you doing here, Remiel?" Ibis twisted to face me fully as he swung his hand toward the window behind me.

"Relishing in life's treasures." I snagged a cigar off the nightstand and struck a match. I inhaled a couple of puffs before throwing myself on the bed and sliding back against the headrest. I gestured at the space beside me. "Care to join?"

"Teslin, really?" Ibis stalked across the room. He yanked the curtain back from the window, peering down at the street below with a scowl. "This place is crawling with debauchery and low-life Magics, Remiel. You don't belong here."

"On the contrary," I countered, wagging the cigar at him as I leaped from the bed. I leaned on the wall opposite him, blowing a plume of smoke in his face. "This is exactly where I belong. It is the same level of activities I used to participate in long before you or Voss walked into my life, except advanced. Riskier. Saucier. Spicier. Magical—"

"You are more than that life, Remiel." Ibis shook his head, staring into me, which sent chills across my skin. "What happened to teaching Magics how to defend themselves against the kingdoms? I would think after what happened in Ghita—"

I shushed him, spittle flying from my mouth as I took a step closer to him. I pinched my thumb and forefinger together, muttering through clenched teeth. "This is a happy place, Ibis. No responsibilities, no baggage, no ambitions. We live to exist and partake in the fruits of this world."

Ibis didn't scowl or flinch. He kept a neutral face as he decreased the space between us, our chests pressing together. He slipped both of his hands on either side of my neck, his thumbs anchoring my head in place.

My mind whirled, and I was thrown back into the cave again, on the day the world stopped turning.

He tilted his head as he narrowed his golden eyes, his warmth radiating from him and wrapping around my chilled, frozen heart. My chest loosened, and my heart started to thaw.

"Remiel." Ibis's thumb twitched against my cheek, caressing, and my eyes fluttered. "You are worth so much more than this life. You always have been, and I have come to bring you back. Leave all this behind—"

"That is the problem with you," I snapped, nudging him away. I snickered then, a maniacal sound, allowing the ice to encase my heart again. "You think it's so easy to just stop caring and leave all that matters behind you, to give up your morality and sell it to the kingdom willing to pay the most. I *refuse* to be like you and Voss."

"That's not what I'm saying," Ibis shouted, splaying both of his hands out in front of him. "You are worth more than rotting away in this cesspool—"

"I don't want to hear how much I'm *worth*." I spat on the floor beside my feet. I pointed the cigar at him, pinched between my fingers. "I am not coming back with you so that Voss can shape me into a soulless, loveless creature who does the bidding of a royal kingdom that would rather see me dead anyway."

"What's the difference between being a soulless, loveless creature there or here?" Ibis said, his face drawn tight. "At least with Voss, you'll have—"

"You?" I chuckled, taking a long drag of the cigar and rolling my eyes as I blew it out. "Even if you would let me love you, living in Voss's world, we don't get to have each other. His rules, remember? What do you think will happen when our apprenticeship ends? We'll run off and live happily ever after?"

Ibis blinked rapidly, his eyebrows pressing together as his mouth parted, and my heart stirred in my chest at the emotions warring on his precious face. Every part of me screamed to reach out to him, to take him into my arms, but I didn't want to torture myself anymore by having him for even a moment.

I wouldn't lose again.

"Please, Remiel," Ibis whispered, rubbing his fingers against his temple. "Let's go grab a coffee, sober you up a little. We can talk more about why I've come when you've got a clearer head—"

"Just get out, Ibis." I sighed, waving my hand to the door. He didn't move, didn't even budge, so I lunged for him and shoved him with a bit of power. "I said get the fuck out!"

Ibis squeezed the doorknob in his hands, yanking the door open. He took one last glance over his shoulder at me, his face burning with the million things I knew he wanted to say. Instead, he shook his head with a huff and slammed the door behind him.

I backed up against the wall beside the window and shut my eyes, allowing the cold, dark claws to pull me back under as I slid to the floor.

Chapter 12

The sun was barely peeking through the window when my door burst open for the second time in sixteen hours. I swore under my breath and squinted against the light seeping in from the hallway sconces. A hulking mass leapt across the room.

"Ibis!" I screamed, trying to scramble away but getting trapped in the sheets and underneath his body instead. "What the actual *fuck* are you doing?"

Ibis didn't say anything as he wrapped a firm hand around my forearm and dragged me out of the bed where I hit the cold wooden floor with a *thunk*. I tried to rip my arm from his grasp, but it only encouraged him. He tightened his grip as he hauled me across the floor towards the window.

"Ibis!" I shouted again, trying to rouse him out of whatever bloodlust stupor he seemed to be absorbed in. "This is not how you say good morning to a friend."

He still didn't answer or even acknowledge that I was lucid as he unlatched the window and shoved it as wide as it would go.

"Maybe some fresh air would do you good..." I trailed off, gaping at him in horror as he clambered onto the windowsill with my arm still in hand. He finally honed his attention onto where I lay on the floor in a twisted, awkward position—his face stern.

"Incentive," was all he said before he jumped out the window, pulling me with him.

We free-fell for a moment, the scenery a blur of grays and browns, before I heard the familiar snap of his wings mixed with the rushing of wind when we lurched upwards. My arm cried out as it was nearly ripped from its socket by the force of gravity and the shift in our momentum. I continued to dangle in Ibis's hand as he soared through the sky towards the Red River, which split the two Teslin towns down the middle.

"I swear to the fucking Gods, Ibis, this is not how you get someone's attention," I called from where I swung in the air below him, but he didn't look down at my screaming. I tried calling his name over and over again, but his set jaw and determined frown told me it took every ounce of effort not to retort back.

Hanging over the Red River, my stomach dropped. Ibis stopped moving, his wings beating with my heart as his hand started to loosen.

I glared with a finger pointed at him, but just as I opened my mouth to argue or plead or negotiate, he *winked* and dropped me into the brown, murky water below.

Dropping some ten- or fifteen-feet head-first into the ice-cold water, I tried to keep every crevice closed as my body submerged below the surface. The chill from the water sunk into my bones, shocking my body. Every muscle tightened as the cold wrapped around me like a familiar embrace, scratching against me as it tried to swallow me deeper.

When my lungs started to burn, I kicked my legs as hard as I could, fascinated by how deep I'd gotten when it took nearly every ounce of effort and whatever air I had left in my lungs to get me above the water. The minute my nose and mouth were free in the open, I swallowed in the air with an audible gasp.

I frantically wiped away the water clinging to my lashes, searching through blurred vision for a stone stairwell because I couldn't imagine using my wings to get out of this situation. Snagging a stone walkway that dipped into the water like a boat loading station, I did my best to paddle through the water, considering I really wasn't sure how one swam.

"Have you lost your fucking mind?" I screamed as I neared, still panting from lack of oxygen and overexertion. I crawled up the slope, glaring up at Ibis, who stood at the top where it met the sidewalk. "What in the ever-loving Gods do you think you're doing?"

Ibis stood like a statue with his arms crossed, so still I questioned if he was even breathing. That only fueled my anger more, rage building from deep within me and spreading across my limbs as my power sparked in my veins.

"Trying to knock some sense into you," Ibis grumbled, waving at the river. "In this case, *shock* some sense into you."

"What sort of sense, bird boy?" I squealed, straightening to full height. "We're barely out of winter, and you think pneumonia is going to bring me to the light?"

He shrugged as if it didn't bother him that I was dripping wet in the chill morning. "Whatever it will take to wake you up."

"I awoke when you burst through my door!" I stomped up the walkway until we were a foot apart, snarling. "Why did you even come here, Ibis? What the hell was the entire point of you coming here? I was content with the path I'd chosen, don't you understand?"

Something deep and dark flashed in his eyes then, and while part of me wanted to crumble at what I thought was hurt, I was already wet, cold, and pissed off.

"I lost them, Ibis," I roared, throwing my hands up. "My family was murdered, and I wasn't there to help them. And I probably could've, which is the worst thing that I have to live with. They're gone, and it's probably my fault."

"Never under any circumstance is it your fault," Ibis frowned, his voice tender. "What in your right mind makes you think it is?"

"I saw those men that day!" My voice cracked at the end as the emotions burned in my throat. "I saw them in that fucking alleyway, doing weird shit in town, and I didn't say anything. I could've even stayed to help protect the Magics there, but for some Godsdamn reason, I brushed it off like everything else."

My chest rose and fell with my breaths, which still hadn't returned to normal from my swim before I started shouting at Ibis. He watched me with an uncharacteristically downturned expression.

"I don't understand why you've come," I whispered, shaking my head, droplets flying around us from my hair. "It was a pointless trip and effort."

The same hurt from earlier brightened the golden hues in his eyes as he set his jaw, the muscles flexing as he pressed his lips in a straight line. He lifted a fist between us but hesitated and dropped it back down.

I raised a lazy eyebrow at him. "You going to beat some sense into me now—"

"You told me to come find you!" Ibis screamed, tears rimming the edges of his eyes. "When I got the chance, I came and found you. And I came and found a shell of the man I fell in love with, fist deep in some bitch's cunt."

I startled, my mouth dropping open as I took a step back. Water dripped into my face, but I was too stunned to brush it away as I shivered in the chill Teslin air.

First of all, Ibis swore, quite filthy words if I do say.

Second of all, he listened, and he came and found me.

But most importantly…

"Love?" I gasped, my breath stopping with that word. "I thought you hated me. Or at least I thought maybe you started to like me, and I left, and I thought then you *definitely* hated me—"

"Oh, trust me, Remiel…" Ibis grabbed my biceps, hauling me against his warm chest with my hands pinned between us. He lowered his face to mine until there was only an inch between our lips. "I wanted to hate you with everything in me. You are terribly crass and have little to no regard for your own existence. Everything you do is effortless, yet you refuse to apply yourself. I work tirelessly for the things that just fall into your lap, and yet you still can't be roused to care."

"I don't know if—"

"You frustrate me to no possible end." Ibis breathed in, pressing our foreheads together. "But Godsdamnit if I don't love you endlessly."

The cold walls that had grown around my heart cracked, allowing his intensity to seep into the cracks. The familiar claws tickled at my mind, reminding me of all the odds stacked against us, of the pain that came from losing anyone I loved.

But I threw the fight and reason out the window, gripping his stupid vest in my hands and slamming my lips against his.

A spark shot through my body, and what was left of my soul split in half, only to be reforged with Ibis, his content groan echoing through me. In an instant, the isolation I'd suffered all my life burnt out as his light cast a glow across every dark crevice within me.

His soft, supple lips moved around mine, and I drank him in like he was the very life force I needed to survive any longer. His hands slipped to the back of my neck, grasping onto any loose strands as I drew mine down his body and gripped his sides, fisting the fabric.

It was like coming home.

Ibis was home.

We slowly pulled away from each other, but we kept our bodies close as my shivering ceased in his presence. I huffed out a laugh, leaning into him.

"If it wasn't clear yesterday," I paused, swallowing against the depth of what I'd felt for him for so long. "I may have loved you from the moment I met you. Every time you kicked my ass, I just fell deeper and deeper."

The most beautiful smile lifted up his cheeks, lighting up his face and adding a twinkle to those amber depths. He planted a quick kiss on my lips, but not before he snagged enough of my bottom lip to drag his sharp canine, sending a thrill through me.

"Let's get you dry," Ibis whispered between us, taking my hand in his.

Ibis sat on the bed in the room I'd been renting and prepared a sort of picnic on top of the sheets as I changed out of my stiff, still-damp clothes and washed off whatever clung to my skin from the murky depths of the Red River. When I emerged from the cramped washroom in just a pair of slacks and a towel draped over my head, Ibis's eyes snagged onto me instantly, then trailed down my body and back up again.

I smirked at him, even as my cock twitched in my pants, and what could only be described as butterflies flapped away in my chest.

Ibis rolled his eyes and suppressed his own smile, gesturing at the space on the mattress in front of him. "Just sit down, Remiel."

I shrugged nonchalantly, tossing the towel onto the floor. Ibis inspected me as I walked across the room to the mattress, but I caught his gaze on my curly mess of damp hair, and his face softened.

"Sometimes your carelessness is enviable," Ibis chuckled, tearing off a piece of a pastry and plopping it into his mouth.

"You know how to loosen up if that's what you're getting at." I accepted the other from him, tilting my head to the side. "I've seen it come out in you plenty of times. When you're cooking, when you're flying, when you're perched up on the highest branch—"

"Remiel," Ibis laughed, rolling his eyes. As it died off, his face slowly bent into a frown. He kept his attention on the pile of bread between us. "I realized a lot of things after you left…"

I waited for him to collect his thoughts, nibbling on the croissant. So many different emotions crossed his face, with an eyebrow twitch here or a clench of his jaw there. I wanted to reach out and console him, and for a moment, I didn't until his face shifted into what could be akin to regret.

I reached across the space and wrapped my hand around his, gently stroking my thumb. His head snapped up to me, and the tension in his face faded.

Just like it had when I'd walked out of the washroom.

Just like it did when he cooked or flew or perched.

"When we talked about what you wanted to do with your future," Ibis began, flipping his hand so our fingers intertwined, "the world I'd come to know and believe in started to change. I'd never thought about using my abilities and knowledge to help others defend themselves so that Magics could live safely at the bare minimum.

"After you left and word got back to Voss and me that you had indeed lost your family, I knew you weren't coming back." Those eyes glistened again with rare tears. "It crushed me more than I thought it would, and that's when I knew I had come to truly care for you and love you. But Voss said that you'd made your choice and that it was best to let you go. It made me angry for a little bit because how could you? How could you give up everything you'd been building, our ambitions, *your* ambitions… Me."

He sighed, his shoulders slumping inward as if he was trying to fold in on himself. His words were a noose around my heart, pinching it with every word, especially as his voice grew quieter toward the end.

I rolled up the towel Ibis had set the food on, moving it to the floor. I grabbed his hands again, pulling him with me to the top of the bed. We lay down, side-by-side, facing one another. I ran my hand lightly up and down his arm, coaxing him through his emotions.

"Voss didn't want to get involved with what happened to Ghita," Ibis said quietly, like it was just as awful to repeat it. "I couldn't leave it alone, though. I needed to know what you saw and what happened, but I also wanted to understand you just a little more. I thought maybe it would help me find you and be able to help when it came time to convince you to come back.

"But when I found out it was a massacre and Etherea was responsible, I started questioning everything I wanted for my future. Everything you had mentioned started to hit harder. Just like you said yesterday, why would I want to work for a kingdom that would more than likely rather see me dead?"

Ibis shifted closer to me, brushing a stray piece of hair from my face and cupping the side of my neck. He rubbed his finger across my stubbled jawline, searching my face.

"I thought about you every night for the last year," Ibis whispered, leaning in and brushing the tip of our noses together. "I would be alone in the cave, and I'd find myself wandering into your room. All your things are still there, so if I closed my eyes, I swore I could hear your laugh or just feel that damn smirk on your face if you walked in and found me there.

"*Like what you see, bird boy?*" Ibis said in a slightly higher-pitched tone, and I busted out laughing at what I guessed was his imitation of me.

I pressed my forehead against him, running my hand up his large bicep and across his now-bare chest, my fingers brushing across the spattering of dark hair there.

"So, what does that mean for you, now?" I asked, running my fingers down the dip of his pecs, slowly following the outline of his abs down his torso. "You know Voss won't allow me back. Who knows if he'll allow you back."

"We'll figure it out," Ibis breathed, even as it hitched when my fingers grazed the top of his pants. "I'd like to think after this long, Voss won't just up and abandon me. We've put too many years in now, and that would mean he'd have to start over and find someone like us to replace me. The old man doesn't have the patience for that."

"I don't know if I want to go back, Ibis," I admitted, lifting my eyes to his. I expected a frown, except there was nothing but unending admiration.

"You could live in Eldamain," Ibis offered, extending his head back. "It's such an easy flight to come find you. That place is packed with Magics that need to be taught to use their gifts and fight and trust each other. You said so yourself, Eldamain could rise up and put a Magic on its throne, fight against The Clips and Etherea."

"You've contemplated *our* future," I chuckled, inching closer so our chests pressed against each other.

But Ibis speaking my dream to me sang in my soul.

"I also heard of this town called Lolis," Ibis explained, dragging his hand over my shoulder and down my back, tracing a line where my wings came out. "It's just on the other side of the Raven's Wood. It seems like they're trying to build a similar community to Ghita."

"That's *in* Etherea." My blood ran cold, and my vision started tunneling.

Ibis caught it, though, and pulled me flush against his body, ripping a quiet gasp from me as he tangled our legs together. "Even more of a reason to go teach them how to defend themselves."

A slow smile climbed up my lips, and I laid my hand flat against Ibis's side, where his ribs met his waist. I urged him toward me, and there was no hesitation as he leaned in. He placed a featherlight kiss against my lips that sent my heart racing, hammering against my chest.

I kissed him back with slight urgency, our mouths moving in tune with each other. He swept his tongue against my bottom lip, eliciting a low growl from my chest. As our tongues danced, his fingers dug into my back as though he could merge us into one.

Just when I thought I would need to lose my pants to relieve some of the pressure against my hardening length, Ibis pulled away.

He curled around me, encasing me in his arms as my body melded perfectly into him. Our breathing synced as we lay there together, and my mind drifted to how our relationship had evolved from the moment I met him to our confessions.

When Voss said it was better to live without attachments in this world, I knew no matter how long I would've stayed at the apprenticeship, there was no future for Ibis and me. Especially how things had been going before I left, I already loved him by then.

But maybe I had been selfish. I wanted to enjoy the moments I did have with him, the flirtations, the fleeting glances, the barely-there caresses, and the lingering looks.

Maybe I just wanted a taste of the sun…

But laying here with him, Ibis poured his heat and warmth into me, and every crevice and inch of me that the darkness had infiltrated burst at the seams with that light.

Chapter 13

After Ibis insisted on paying off all the remaining debt I'd acquired through the Obsidian Coin and Hugo, we wiped the slate clean and flew for the Black Avalanches.

When we passed over Ghita, I wasn't shocked to find the town desolate and abandoned a year after the incident. I almost told Ibis to stop to see my childhood home, but then I regrettably remembered that I had left my family's bodies where they'd been slain.

Ibis must have felt the shift in the air between us because he cleared his throat before saying, "I buried them for you."

I snapped my head up, frowning as I blinked back the tears that instantly sprung to my eyes. "You what?"

Ibis cleared his throat again, keeping his focus directly ahead of us. "I told you I wanted to see for myself what happened. It seemed like people cleaned up the town, but the person who'd told me about the attack mentioned where your home was."

"You saw…" My blood ran cold, and my stomach churned at the images that flashed through my mind.

My father and mother huddled together…

My sister, my best friend…

"I can't imagine what you felt when you saw them." Ibis finally turned his head to me. I expected to find some level of disgust, but I found pity, and I wasn't sure if that felt any better. "I'm not going to divulge anything about the state of your home other than I conducted a proper Echidna burial."

I tried to smile around the pain and tight, heavy pressure in my chest. Ibis offered a soft smile, nodding once in understanding.

"My mother was actually from the House of Argo," I mumbled around the pain, swallowing it down.

"I'm sorry." Ibis frowned, his cheeks tinted pink. "I didn't know—"

"Don't apologize for burying my family, Ibis." I smiled as a little of that pressure eased. "I'm sure she would've preferred to be buried in the customs of my father's house anyway. She didn't have many traits, but that's actually where I get my eyes from."

Ibis scanned my face, a smile gradually lighting up his. "I wish I could've thanked her for that because it has to be one of my favorite things about you."

He focused back on our path, leaving me in the silence again to mull over that compliment. Instead, my mother's beautiful face came to mind, the way her eyes glistened when I'd left for Voss's. For once, her memory didn't bring the pain it had over the last year.

As we descended in front of the entrance of Voss's cave, a whole new level of anxiety returned, knocking the wind out of me as we fell from the sky. I stood back as Ibis walked up to the door, gnawing on my lip with the tip of a canine.

"I feel like I've failed tremendously," I whispered to Ibis, shaking my head as I stared at the concealed cave. "My father got me this apprenticeship with Voss, and I feel like I've completely disappointed him and spit on his name by even daring to come back."

"We're not here to beg for your position back," Ibis assured, reaching for my hand. "You don't have to come in if you don't want. I'll grab your things for you."

My initial instinct was to say no, but the more I thought about facing that laser-sharp stare, the tighter my insides twisted. So, instead of forcing myself into something I truly didn't want to do, I nodded my agreement and let Ibis go in alone.

That's not to say the anxiety left my body the moment he crossed the threshold. It raged within my chest, scratching and clawing with every breath I took until I started to pace back and forth on the path that led to the door.

It wasn't until I heard clamoring and raised voices that I stopped pacing to focus my hearing on what was being said. I took a single step closer to the door, but I remained a few feet away.

"For love, Ibis?" Voss shouted, his voice traveling through the cave like he followed after Ibis. "This isn't about the good of the world or the good of Magics. This is because you are in love, and you are blind!"

"Love is part of it, Voss." Ibis's voice carried similarly to Voss's, but it was strong and firm compared to our mentor's frantic pitch. "But be honest, Voss. You can sit here and claim all you want that you have every kingdom in your grasp for the past one-hundred-and-fifty years, but it is they who have had you at their beck and call, pretending like you have freedom."

"Khonsa above," Voss chuckled darkly, and I could almost see him rubbing his forehead. "Remiel is the one who told you this, isn't he? The boy is a dreamer, Ibis. His mind is in the dark, and he lives with the stars. His parents sheltered him and his sister and look what it got them. At least if you have the ability to work with kingdoms, you ensure your safety—"

"And what about the safety of Magics like Remiel's parents?" Ibis stopped moving. "Not every community can be safe like the one I came from. On the main continent, there is nothing to protect

Magics from their aggressors. I just came from Teslin, where it seems that's the only real place Magics have power outside of being *graced* with a mentor that will give them an in with the kingdoms. What they have to do is *disgusting*, and there has to be another way.

"That's what Remiel dreams of." Ibis's voice moved closer to the door, but he didn't sound close enough to leave yet. "Why can't you see that? You could help so many with the gifts and opportunities you've created."

A deafening silence permeated the air, both inside the cave and surrounding me on the opposite side of the door. I swallowed against my hammering heart, allowing Ibis to handle this fight on his own, even if I wanted to bust down that door and beat the old man for daring to speak about my family.

A family he encouraged me to abandon.

I clenched and unclenched my fists as Voss continued, his voice harsher than I'd ever heard. "I worked for the *opportunities* I have. No one helped me get here. No Magic community, no Great Karasi, no Jorah. If those two want to waste their time and abilities helping Sirians and Magics and trying to sway kingdoms into accepting either Being back into their graces, that's their choice. Until then, I will continue the way I have always conducted business."

Voss's feet shuffled across the stone flooring and stopped roughly where Ibis had.

"You will never live a comfortable life, Ibis. You will fight for the rest of your life to try and protect the people you love. It will be never-ending, and you will scrabble to create a suitable living. Do you believe such an emotion as fleeting as love is worth it?"

Too many heartbeats thumped in the silence within the Black Avalanches as Voss waited for Ibis's answer.

"I've learned a lot from you, Voss," Ibis said in an even tone, "but I think the most important lesson is that without love, there is nothing to fight for. Nothing to die for."

Just seconds after his final declaration, Ibis swung the front door open with two slacks slung over his shoulder, his blazing, deep golden eyes latching onto me. The frantic energy swirling in those depths calmed enough, but his shoulders were stiff, and his face drawn tight.

"Let's get the fuck out of this place," Ibis declared, shocking me again with his swearing. I chuckled to myself at the idea that maybe I was an awful influence on the man, but when I connected with Voss's steel gray eyes, I considered maybe I was a better influence than our mentor.

I slowly lifted my middle finger to my mouth and licked it before launching into the sky after the love of my life.

·⋆˙☽⋆·˖·

I followed Ibis up the narrow staircase, his shoulders still tense from our exit with Voss. I couldn't help the slump of my shoulders and the heavy weight at the pit of my stomach.

Once again, I felt responsibility pushing down on me, a small voice repeating how his anger and tension were all my fault.

The world Voss had fed him was all Ibis had come to know after leaving Riddling, the future he'd planned for himself since he was young. Had I truly been so selfishly blinded by my grief, greed, and love for him that I let him walk away from that?

The silence on the entire trip to some town called Vega in Mariande left an unsettling feeling in my gut. It meant he was deep in thought, and I wondered if he'd reconsidered everything we had planned the previous night, talking until early morning.

We discussed the plan for me to live in Eldamain, connecting with the Great Karasi or building a greenhouse somewhere where the Magics were more spread out. He'd continue his apprenticeship, and I would build up more money for us to top off what his family had given him before he came to the Black Avalanches.

There was even a Plan B if Voss told us to kick rocks, which is exactly what happened. We agreed to fly straight for Lolis, where that small community was growing. We would teach them to protect themselves and contribute to the economy now that I knew some of the herbs, potions, and plants that were hard to come by in Teslin.

Sure, Hugo wasn't the best connection to keep, but anything to help build Magic influence and power that didn't require sleazy methods.

But now, in the silence that continued as we journeyed through the inn, my throat burned at the thought that I would lose Ibis, and he would go home to Riddling.

We stopped in front of a dark wooden door with a golden *12* on it. Ibis stuck the key into the lock, giving me a tight-lipped grin before shoving the door open with his shoulder.

I passed under the frame after him, scanning the very small room before us. A tiny bathroom, no bigger than an outhouse, was tucked into the far corner. A *single* bed lay in the middle, with two wooden tables on either side. Luckily, the bed was designed for two bodies, although there would be no wings present while we slept.

"If you're uncomfortable sharing a bed tonight," I said to the deafening silence, "then I'd understand, and I can always grab my own room."

Ibis stiffened beside the bed where he'd been running his hand over the sheet. He snapped his piercing gaze at me with a startled frown.

"We shared one last night," he explained, pursing his lips. "Why would anything have changed? I thought many things that happened in the last day would have proven how I want to spend as many moments beside you as you'll let me."

Warmth spread through me at his words, my throat burning along with the corners of my eyes. I averted my gaze, staring at a stain on the carpeted floor. I shrugged. "You just lost your apprenticeship because of me. You've risked the future you've worked your entire life for—"

"For you?" Ibis's feet shuffled slowly toward me. He grabbed my jaw between his thumb and forefinger, forcing our gazes to meet. "The future I envisioned for myself when I was younger was conjured by a lonely boy who wanted nothing more than to be loved and accepted."

He gripped my face between both of his hands, his thumbs grazing my temples as his fingers wrapped around the base of my head. He inched his face closer to mine, brushing our noses together. "But life changes, and there is more to life than the roles and the games we play in our world. If I have to choose between a life being at the beck and call of whichever kingdom will have me or a life of simplicity with the man I love..."

He pulled back enough so that I could capture his whole face. He didn't need to answer because I knew. I knew very well by now what he'd choose because if I had to choose between an empty, monotonous life in a pub or being surrounded by love for however long the Gods gave us, I would choose love.

"You look at me like I'm the sun," Ibis whispered, brushing his lips across mine. "But little do you know, you are the moon in my night and half my soul. I am yours, now and forever."

I crashed my lips into his, my palms flattening against the hard planes of his stomach. He moaned softly against me, opening my mouth with his and sweeping his tongue along mine. My legs quivered as he trailed his lips across my cheeks and down my neck, dragging a sharp canine against the sensitive skin.

"Ibis," I whispered into the room, dragging my hands up his broad chest and into the soft ringlets of his hair. I entangled my hands, yanking his head back to look at him again.

I wanted to tell him how much I loved him. I wanted to thank him for saving me, for bringing the light back into my life after the longest, darkest night.

Instead, I pulled his lips back onto mine. He melted against me, bathing me in a heat that loosened my shoulders and tightened my cock. As his hips pressed into me, urging me toward the bed, I felt his hard length press between us.

Once my legs bumped against the mattress, I put some space between us and got to work on the buttons of his stupid vest as he managed to untie the laces of my slacks. After I slid the vest over his chest, I shimmied out of my slacks and flung my shirt over my head.

Standing before each other, I reached out my hand, my fingers lightly tracing the carved muscle that was Ibis. I journeyed down his abdomen until I brushed his *thick* cock, which twitched at my touch. I smirked up at him only to find his gaze drinking in every inch of me.

"You are…" Ibis shook his head, breathless.

I smiled then, both canines exposed to him, as I gripped his forearm and lowered to the mattress. I scooted across the plush surface, enjoying my view as he rustled through his bag and pulled out a clear vial. He gently placed it on the end table before joining me on the bed and crawling toward me as I leaned back on the pillows.

He kept inching towards me until he hovered above, his arms pinning me between them. He lowered for another kiss, his movements languid and gentle as we caressed each other. I reached between us, gripping his length in my hand and pumping him once, reveling in his hips bucking against me. When I reached the tip, I swiped my thumb over the crease.

"So impatient," Ibis mumbled against me, but I felt the smile tugging at his lips. I chuckled breathlessly as one of his hands reached over to the end table.

I dragged my hand down his muscular thigh as he kneeled on top of me, popping the cork from the bottle. He poured a generous amount of the liquid into his hand, coating his cock as he studied me through bated lashes.

"Gods, I've wanted you for too long," I growled, digging my nails into his skin.

All Ibis did was smirk lazily as he gripped my legs and slung them over his shoulders. My stomach coiled in anticipation, my skin buzzing. He aligned himself against me, and I breathed as he slipped inside slowly.

I moaned as pleasure lit a path through me, throwing my head back against the pillow as he pushed all the way in. His throat bobbed, his mouth propping open as he breathed a content sigh, stretching and filling every inch he could.

Ibis gripped my thighs and pulled out, only to thrust in with a little more fever, throwing his head back as he let out a rumbling moan into the room. A shiver went up my spine, the fire within setting me ablaze.

He set a steady pace then, pulling out only to bury himself into me. Our satisfied groans echoed one another with every thrust, teeming with the pleasure that was building.

I gripped his thighs, relishing in the flex of his muscles as he rocked in and out at a steady pace. I smirked up at him, calling out one of my claws and scraping them down the sensitive skin on his inner thighs.

Ibis hissed, flashing his canines at me, which only had me thickening as cum leaked from my tip. In one expert and extremely intoxicating movement, Ibis grabbed my thigh in his hand and flipped me onto my knees without removing himself.

I propped onto my forearms so I could entirely bear myself to him, groaning as he thrust into me at a deeper angle, hitting new points that were like sparks along my skin. I prickled as heat spread to every limb.

He continued his tantalizing pace but reached in front of me and wrapped his warm hand around my cock, his hand still slick with the lubricant he'd applied to himself. He expertly worked my shaft up and down, pumping in time with the grinding of his hips.

Every sensation heightened, teeming with the pressure building low inside of me.

"Fuck, Ibis," I hissed in between my teeth.

He hunched over me, his firm chest pressing against my back. His breath grazed my ear as he demanded, "Beg for it."

I twisted my head so our lips brushed, slipping my hand around his where he held my dick in his hand. I growled, "Fuck me harder, Ibis."

My own command sparked something in what I could see of his golden hues, and he snapped his hips harder and faster, just as I said. The further he buried himself into me, stretching me, it felt as though our souls finally melded together in a swirl of light and dark.

It didn't take long for both of us to find release then, and I soared over the edge when Ibis's pace slowed, fire rippling through me.

We fell to bed together, and Ibis cuddled into me, burying his face into the crook of my neck with heavy breaths.

"That was—" He paused, his lips brushing my neck. "More than I imagined it could be."

I grabbed a fist full of his hair, unable to help myself, as I chuckled darkly with a smirk. "Oh, so you dreamt of fucking me?"

I didn't think it was possible, but Ibis turned beat red as his eyes flickered around the room, anywhere but me. They stopped moving at something above my head, and he painfully dragged them back to me with a serious face drawn. "Since the time I pinned you beneath me, I found myself… thinking about it."

I startled a little, inclining my head to look at him better. "That long ago? That was within the first few months of me being there."

"It was purely attraction initially since it'd been a while for me." Ibis shook his head, blinking. "But it started to evolve to more when you came home from visiting your family…"

"Always so serious." I pressed my lips gently to his, muttering against them, "I love you, my sun."

Ibis smiled against me, brushing a stray hand of dark hair from my forehead. "I love you, my soul."

CHAPTER 14

END OF SUMMERTIDE 1789 A.V.

Over 4 Years Later

I gazed out the window above the sink, my arms crossed over my chest. From here, I watched the young children play a game of catch, one of the bouncing blond heads belonging to my friend Willem's daughter, who lived a few homes down. She squealed as another child almost snagged the skirt of her dress, but she twisted out of their grasp in time for them to tumble to the ground as she made a beeline for her home.

A soft, breathy chuckle left me as I smirked, shaking my head at the cunning maneuver I'd just witnessed.

Firm hands slipped onto my shoulders and down my arms before bracing the counter on either side of me. I leaned back into Ibis's solid chest, my lower back tingling at the graze of his canines along my neck.

He placed a gentle kiss on top of the spot he bit last night, muttering, "I've caught you watching the children play for the seventh day in a row, Remiel. Is there something you'd like to discuss, or are they truly that intriguing to you?"

"There's a few reasons I watch them." I shrugged nonchalantly, but my chest tightened. "The first is that they remind me of my childhood. Cara and I lived like this, in a Magic community with other Magic children. The second is that Lila is too smart for her own good, and I love watching her outwit the others."

"Because that, too, reminds you of Cara?" Ibis guessed, gently twisting me around. He scanned my face with skepticism. "Is that all?"

I pressed my lips together, unable to meet his gaze as I forced out, "Did you ever envision your future with children?"

"You mean, did I envision being a father?" He took a few steps back to lean against the kitchen island. He braced his hands behind him, shrugging. "When I thought I'd be an agent to the kingdoms, I dreamed of a life more similar to that of Voss or the Great Karasi."

"A bachelor." I smirked, but it was half-assed. The swirling in my stomach burned, biting at my nerves as I waited for him to continue.

"I suppose." He tilted his head as a soft smile climbed up his cheeks, lighting up his eyes. "The minute I fell in love with you, my life changed for the better. And the last four years we've spent expanding this community and building our life together, the grander life seems it can be."

"So, is that a…?" I trailed off, wincing into my shoulder as I shut one eye.

He snatched my forearm in his grip and hauled me to his chest. He grabbed my chin with his other hand. "I think fatherhood could suit us both beautifully one day. But for now, I want to take my time with you, just as I did last night."

I swallowed against his deep, seductive voice rumbling against my chest, my cock twitching at the memory of him taunting me with his agonizing touch, his lips, his teeth…

"We cannot expose children to such revelry," I whispered, our breath tangling between us.

Ibis hummed, snaking a hand around my lower back—

A knock on the door startled both of us, and I even yelped, "For the love of the *Gods*."

Ibis laughed, throwing his head back as he peeled me off him before making his way to our front door.

"Don't tell me you're about to answer that door at *full* attention, Ibis," I shouted after him, which caused him to stumble on his way to the door. I chuckled darkly as he grabbed the doorknob and shook his head, swinging it open.

My mouth dropped in horror at the child that stood in our doorway coupled with her father's hands braced on her shoulders, his lip curled at me over Ibis's shoulder.

"Willem!" Ibis shouted overenthusiastically, shooting me a brief look over his shoulder. "And lovely Lila. What can I do for you two this morning?"

"Did you know it's my mom's birthday today?" Lila squeaked, twisting the ends of her long, ash-blond hair between her two hands. She blinked her beady brown eyes up at Ibis. "Will you and Remy come over to our plot to celebrate? We'll be decorating the patio with dyed strips of parchment and ribbons!"

"We would be happy to celebrate," Ibis agreed, nodding once. "Maybe Remiel has some extra flowers from the garden he can contribute to the celebration."

"Mm," was all I managed from the kitchen, leaning on the island.

"What else were you going to ask, Lila?" Willem urged with a small grin.

Her eyes widened, flickering from her father to Ibis to me and then back to Ibis again. She motioned for him to bend down to her height, where she cupped her tiny hand around his ear and whispered something.

Ibis slowly rose from his hunch, eyeing her suspiciously as she squirmed impatiently, but a smile broke across his face, and he nodded once.

The squeal of delight that burst from that child damn near blew my eardrum.

"I'll be right back," Ibis said to me with a wink before scooping her up in his arms and stepping just outside the door onto our patio. I saw a brief flash of white, accompanied by a woosh, before he launched with her into the sky.

"She wanted to go flying again?" I asked with a smile, busying my hands with some of the leftover dishes from breakfast.

Willem chuckled under his breath, stepping into the house. "Every other day at this point between the both of you. Let's hope the Gods gift her with feathered wings like your husband for your sakes and for the world's should they face her wrath."

"I don't think I've asked if you and Theresa are both from the House of Nemea." I briefly glanced at him as he sat at the dining table.

He nodded, more of a slow wave-like movement with his head as he clicked his tongue against the roof of his mouth. "Yeah, but neither of us have any special abilities. I have retractable claws and fangs, but she only has the fangs."

"Well, with Lila's love of flight," I chuckled to myself, throwing the last dish into the sink, "she's bound to have wings."

The silence from Willem was slightly unnerving, so I quickly peered over my shoulder. He stared off toward our living space in the middle of the room, his face scrunched apprehensively.

"What's on your mind, friend?" I asked, twisting around and resting on the counter with my arms crossed over my chest.

Willem blinked away whatever thoughts occupied his mind. He opened and closed his mouth a few times like he'd been debating whether or not to bring said thoughts up. He finally sighed heavily before relenting. "I was in the main square getting some meats from the butcher, and I passed a strange sight. I wanted to run it by you because I heard you've had experience with… intruders."

I furrowed my brow deep, the skin pressing together in the middle. I extended my head out in front of me. "Intruders? As in… I'm not sure what you mean."

"They didn't appear to be Magics," Willem explained, resting an elbow on the table. "They were walking up and down allies, and just everything about the way they were slinking through buildings sent warning bells off in my head."

"What did they look like?" I asked, pushing off the counter. My heart started pounding in my ribcage, my stomach hollowing out.

"They looked very average with your standard Etherean garb on." Willem shrugged, but the more he explained, the louder the blood roared in my ears. "They kept muttering to one another, huddled together, waving their arms up and down a building or down an alley—"

"When they motioned towards different directions…" I paused, swallowing against the pressure in my chest, bracing an arm on the island. My voice came out hoarser than intended. "Can you show me how they did it? *Exactly* how they did it, not general movements."

Willem shot me a sidelong glance through narrowed eyes, but he did what I asked. He faced me head-on and lifted his arm at a perfect angle, stiffly swinging it up and down. He pointed his two fingers and thumbs as he indicated up and down the wall. "Some sort of hand symbol like that. Does it mean something to you?"

I drummed my fingers across the wooden surface of the counter, gnawing at my lip and the burning in my lungs. My breath started coming in short bursts as I shook my head fiercely and wagged a finger at him.

"Those are military gestures." I stormed for our door, my leather wings bursting from my back as I shimmied them out. Willem's face revealed nothing short of awe and intrigue, but I couldn't pay attention to that. "If they were in casual Etherean garb using military gestures, those were members of the Etherean army."

I swung the door open and tucked my wings, pausing at the threshold as I glanced back at him and added, "If we have the Etherean military scoping out our town, we need to be prepared."

.⋆✶.☽.✦⋆.

I sat in the middle of the grass within the circle of homes, one arm propping me up and the other resting over my bent knee with a glass of whiskey dangling precariously from my fingertips. My eyes kept flitting over the entire town gathered in our area for Theresa's birthday, studying faces and monitoring suspicious behavior.

But everything went as it usually did for a birthday in Lolis. Some of the more musically inclined played their instruments in front of a small bonfire constructed by none other than Ibis and Willem, with children, women, and men dancing around it to the beat of the drum.

"You need to relax, Remiel," Ibis cut through my focus, sitting beside me. He handed me a skewer of meat that Willem had cooked over the fire, urging me to take it. "Enjoy the evening."

"I'm worried," I explained through the side of my mouth, keeping my voice low. "I know how those fuckers operate. I'd dealt with enough of them when I was younger. After Ghita, I know better than to ignore signs that they're scoping our town."

"You also didn't see them yourself," Ibis mumbled around a mouthful of food, sticking the skewer directly in my face. My stomach rumbled at the smell that wafted around me. "You haven't eaten since this morning, and you've been flying between here, the woods, and Eryphus all day. Not eating isn't going to help you any."

I glared at him from the corner of my eyes, but I melted when I laid my eyes upon him.

His face was soft and serene, eyes blazing in the setting sun like the whiskey in my glass, swirling with a golden depth that never failed to take my breath away. The glowing light cast a luminescent sheen across his golden skin, cutting at the sharp angles of his stunning jawline.

His lips twitched in tune with mine, spreading into a joyful grin as I fought my own smile. I rolled my eyes, snatching the skewer from his hand and ripping off a chunk of meat.

"I'm glad we've come to an agreement." Ibis smirked, extending his long, cut legs out in front of him and leaning back on his hands. He turned his face up to the sky, soaking in the final warmth of daylight.

"It's not fair when, with one look from you, I am thoroughly dazzled into submission," I grumbled as I took another bite, even more aware of the biting hunger from a day of traveling back and forth. I mumbled around the chunk, "I feel like I'm at a disadvantage constantly. It's a wonder you love me."

"And yet, I do." He turned his smile back on me, his eyes crinkling at the corners. "Every anxious, protective, dark, and maybe a little pale part of you."

A single hack of laughter burst from me, melding with his. I shook my head as Ibis continued to find amusement at his own joke, leaning to one side as he used his other hand to rub at his bare abdomen.

My smile and bliss faded quickly, though, as I watched Willem haul his wife to his lap, burying his face into her neck. Beside them was Dahlia, respectfully holding hands with Willem's eldest daughter—who'd just turned eighteen this past summer—tucking a strand of hair behind her ear.

I had to admit, another version of me would've given Dahlia a lot of shit for waiting two years to be with her, but watching Ibis smile at the people around us…

I knew waiting for the love of your life was always worth every moment with them.

"I think we should leave," I blurted quietly, barely above a whisper, but I knew both of us had hearing strong enough to pick up on it.

"Remiel." Ibis's head snapped to me, the frown on his face mixed with shock. "Why?"

"If those were Ethereans—" I stopped myself, my gaze flickering across the multitude of children this community had inherited. The number of families we held in our city. "If those were Ethereans, we don't stand a chance. These are *families*, Ibis. You and I are the only ones trained to fight them, and they will travel in numbers you and I cannot battle alone."

"That's more of a reason to stay, Remiel." Ibis slid his hand on top of mine, leaning closer. "You are not the helpless boy you were when you appeared on Voss's doorstep. You trained with him for nearly two years, and we've kept up our sparring for the last four years since. We've been training Willem, Dahlia, and Roger, not to mention those who started this month."

"I'm worried we don't have enough time to train more." My eyes caught on Willem's oldest daughter again, Maddie, as she picked up Lila and lifted her onto her shoulders with Dahlia's assistance.

"We have to stay and help as much as we can," Ibis insisted, snagging my chin with his freehand. He drew my gaze to him, studying my face. "You care for these people. Do you really think you could just up and leave them entirely defenseless?"

No. I couldn't.

I could never leave the weak undefended, not the way my hometown had been left untrained and undefended.

I bit my lip, tears burning the back of my eyes. I couldn't fathom losing any of the people around me, but I couldn't fathom losing Ibis more.

"We'll stay," I whispered. He palmed my cheek, and I leaned into his embrace. "But if we feel like there is nothing more we can do, we go."

"Okay." Ibis nodded once, his hand slipping from my face. We both faced the crowd of people again, watching Dahlia and Maddie dance around the fire with Lila on the latter's shoulders.

"If we get separated," I added, fighting past the tightness in my throat, "because that could happen, then we need a place to meet."

"It would be better if we partnered with any beginners." The gold of Ibis's eyes winked as the sun set beyond the horizon, dusk spreading across the sky. "And this is all only to say *if* something were to come from the men Willem saw. We can meet at The Raven's Wood."

"And how will we find each other?" I stared at him in the glow of the bonfire, basking in his warmth and letting it settle into me to calm my still-racing nerves.

"I'd be able to find you in the darkest night." Ibis smiled, squeezing my hand trapped between his and the grass. "Even in the afterlife."

"And in the next life." I scooted into him, our shoulders

brushing. I laid my head on his shoulder and let his light engulf me.

Chapter 15

Midwinter 1790 A.V.

4 Months Later

By the time I finished my meeting with Hugo and errands in Rian, night had already descended. Even without my night vision, a small smile tugged at the corners of my lips as the fluffy tops of the Raven's Wood trees came into view as I flew closer to Lolis.

As much as I didn't want to leave Lolis with little defense, I had to go to Rian to make the trade with Hugo. He wanted his hallucinogenic plants, and I wanted the money to support our community and the plants from Teslin that could only grow in their humidity. I had even argued with Ibis for almost an hour about why he should come with me, while Ibis countered that it was better for him to stay back in the town just in case, and I relented.

Which was why I was now flying back so damned late.

Approaching Lolis, I realized what I thought were the fluffy tops of the trees in Raven's Wood were opaquer, especially when I remembered it was far too late for the Magics of Lolis to be wide awake with torches.

I tilted my trajectory, tucking my wings closer, as I quickly plummeted to the ground. Billowing smoke rose high into the air, lingering above buildings doused in flames.

I hit the ground with a heavy thud, and the sound around me swallowed me up. The crackling wood of homes eerily reminded me of a bonfire, barely concealing the faint screams echoing from every direction, names called in desperation.

My heartbeat hammered against my chest as I discarded my satchel, staring in horror at the hut before me.

Our hut. Our home.

The roof entirely caved in, embers and flames waving into the dark night.

"No," I breathed, running straight to it. I jogged around the perimeter, wondering if I would hear any sign of life or if I was too late.

I refused to believe I had once again been too late.

I didn't know what I expected to find while the fire ate at my home and all the memories that lay within its walls. I thought about the other day on our lawn, wrapped in Ibis's embrace as we watched the stars chase each other across the sky. An image of the children chasing each other on the green flashed in my head, and I glanced over my shoulder only to find the grass's charred remains and the homes burning across the way.

As I neared my home, I stumbled in my stride when I remembered the conversation on the lawn a few months back about the Etherean men, and my blood ran cold.

Gods, I'd been right, and I let Ibis convince me that we could stay.

I cursed under my breath, trying to peer into a window, reminding myself now was not the time to be frustrated with Ibis over something that I couldn't care less about at that moment.

I just cared about finding him, and my heart jumped into my throat at the pessimistic questions whispering in my mind.

Like what if I couldn't find him? What if he was trapped inside the house? What if he was—

"Ibis!" I shouted, but it morphed into a scream as the red and orange flames roared through the window, the sweat on my head evaporating.

I stared up at the stars above me, collecting my frantic, racing thoughts and slowing my wild heart. I took deep breaths like Ibis instructed, closing my eyes. I tapped into my enhanced senses, listening to every little sound around me.

Crumbling wood. Somebody calling for their mother. A woman calling for more water. The paws of a creature escaping the mayhem. Willem whaling—

"Willem?" I yelled into the wreckage that was Lolis, lurching upright. I tried to count the houses around me, discerning walls and piles of burning wood to find the one that would be his.

There, a couple of yards away from what should've been his front porch, Willem crouched over three unmoving lumps on the ground.

"Fucking Gods," I gasped, scrambling to my feet and sprinting across the distance between us.

I stood beside him, watching him brush the matted, bloodied hair away from who looked like Lila. Her beautiful, ash—blonde hair almost looked copper now, and my stomach churned at the indent on the side of her head.

"Willem…" I tried to lay my hand on his shoulder, but he shrugged me off, snarling like the feral man he was. Based on the state of the other two bodies, I knew that Theresa and Maddie suffered similar fates as Lila, and I couldn't help the tears that escaped my burning eyes.

"Willem," I said again, more forceful. "What the hell happened?"

"Those mother fuckers," Willem growled, drawing Lila closer

into his body and resting his chin on top of her mangled head. "Fucking Ethereans. Why? Why did they have to come here? We weren't hurting anybody. We just wanted to exist in peace. The children—Gods, my children, Remy. Look at my children… Theresa."

I pressed my lips together, trying to fight the rising bile from overwhelming decay and charred bodies around me. All I could see in my head now was Ibis, beaten and bloodied by those who harmed the rest of this Gods-forsaken town. I threw the thoughts and memories of my sister out of my head, focusing on finding him first.

I just needed to find Ibis.

"Remy!" a feminine voice shouted, and I looked up in time to catch Dahlia in my arms, the smell of smoke emanating off her suffocating me. I peeled her away, holding her at arm's length.

She was covered head-to-toe in soot, her red eyes eerily peeking out from beneath the muck. Her hair was pulled into a braid, but so many pieces had escaped, stuck to her face with what looked like sweat and blood.

"Fuck, Dahlia," I snarled, swiping a thick streak of something that resembled sludge off her face. "Willem said—"

"There were some of those—" A hacking cough burst from her, and she bent over with a hand on her chest. I shifted on my feet as she recovered, wincing. "The guys that were here a few months back had a shit load of others with them. They were dressed in street clothes, but they all sounded Etherean."

"Knights," I growled, curling a lip. I threw my hands on top of my head, my vision tinting red as I yanked on the strands of my hair.

"They just started throwing buckets of oil on everything." Her voice wavered as she bit back tears. "Some were throwing buckets while others were torching every building. Anything they couldn't set on fire, they just started killing by whatever means they brought. Swords, fists, arrows…"

I shut my eyes at the images that flashed across my mind of Cara, beaten and bruised nearly beyond recognition. I didn't have words for the burning, aching sensation crawling its way up my chest and into my throat, so I just let it out with a raw scream.

Dahlia flinched at my sudden outburst. I cut off the sound with a hand down my face, the other hooking onto my hip. I angled my hand between us, about to say something, but her eyes found Willem and his family at our feet.

Her love at her feet.

A strangled wail trembled from her lips before she could slap her hand over her mouth at the sight of Maddie. She mumbled around her hand, "Oh, Gods. Willem…"

Dahlia knelt beside Maddie and Theresa's bodies, hovering a shaking hand over Maddie's once-blonde hair. When her fingertips grazed her forehead, Dahlia burst into tears, throwing herself protectively over the gaping hole in Maddie's chest cavity.

"Dahlia," I whispered, cursing myself at interrupting her mourning. But I was desperate, and I needed to know. "Have you seen Ibis?"

Dahlia hiccupped around a sob, and my chest clenched as she attempted to collect herself over the loss of her love. I pressed my lips together, shutting my eyes to try and calm my turbulent heart and mind.

"We were separated quickly," she managed quietly, petting Maddie's hair back as tears streamed down her face. "I'm sorry. I'm not sure what happened…"

Her lower lip trembled, and I knew I wouldn't get anywhere else with her on the matter.

"Did you see Ibis, Willem?" I asked as I sank to the ground and carefully crawled before him to not disturb Lila in his arms.

But I could've been a ghost for all Willem cared. He kept rocking his daughter back and forth in his arms while his gaze flickered between his other child in front of Dahlia and his wife just a few feet away from us.

"Willem!" I snapped, grabbing his dirt and blood-streaked face roughly between my hands. "Willem! Where the *fuck* is my husband?"

"How should I know?" he screamed, shoving my shoulder hard enough to send me on my ass. "After they attacked my family, I couldn't give two fucks about the rest of this Godsdamn shithole."

I wiped the gravel from my palms as I towered over him, my heart cracking for him and a weight dropping into my stomach.

Not for the fate of my own family, his sanity, or the tenderness that was Dahlia, but for what every Magic here would suffer from for the rest of their lives.

The heavy, bone-deep isolation.

I glanced around, turning in a slow circle, as I watched the remnants of the town burn to the ground around me. Even the already faint screams had quieted, which was never good. I heard distant whimpers mixed in with the settling blazes, the whoosh of buckets desperately throwing water to staunch the madness.

Another Magic town, broken by Etherea, with no one to help.

A shot of lightning raced through my veins, jolting me. My hand flew to my chest, where my frantic heart was still beating, remembering more from the initial conversation with Ibis a few months back.

The Raven's Wood.

I took flight briefly over Lolis to not only reach the forest quicker, but I also wanted a higher view of the damage done. There wasn't a doubt in my mind that those men had, in fact, been Etherean knights scoping out Lolis on behalf of their king. The events of then and today were startlingly like the events of the death of my family, which only caused the chill in my bones to ache deeper the longer I didn't have Ibis beside me.

I stood at the edge of the tree line, my eyes sweeping over the unburnt bark and leaves dangling precariously from their branches. If I looked close enough, it seemed like the trees swayed inward and hunched, putting as much distance from the fires ravaging Lolis and concealing themselves from the horrors inflicted on the Magics.

I tuned out the noise of the fires and the faded conversation and cries, focusing my hearing on the quiet din of The Raven's Wood. I listened past the birds flapping, animals scurrying, and trees creaking, searching for something that was amiss.

A soft whimper tickled at my senses, and I ran into the thicket without another thought.

Deep into the forest, I followed the moans and soft, unintelligible murmurs, my heart beating harder in my throat the louder they got. When I turned around a rather tight collection of trees, nothing could've prepared me for what I saw.

Nailed between two thick trees, Ibis hung by his wings, spread wide on either side of him. The cartilage was bent at all sorts of awful angles that made my back twinge, clumps of feathers missing to expose the bare skin underneath. What was left of those beautiful, white feathers dripped in blood, still fresh from the leaking wounds where the arrows impaled him onto the trees.

I shivered at the sight, my feet glued to the ground beneath me, even if I felt like I was floating into a dark nothingness.

"*Nychterída*," Ibis managed, his head hanging. He sputtered, deep red blood bubbling over his lips and dribbling down his chin.

His old nickname for me and the blood forced me out of my stupor, and I closed the distance between us, grasping his slack head and forcing him to meet my eyes. Those normally golden hues were dim and dull, his lids heavy with the effort to stay conscious.

"What have you managed to get yourself into?" I whispered, tears gathering in the corners of my eyes. I brushed his own away with my thumb, shaking my head. "Ibis, love. What do you say we get you down?"

"Watch for—" he winced, a shudder running through him. "All the arrows."

"I think I can manage," I assured with a soft smile, but he shook his head in my hands, his face contorting.

"Not the wings." He sputtered again, his blood spattering across my face. I startled, arching my body back as I kept his head in my hands and peered between us.

The world stopped around me as my vision tunneled in on the three arrows protruding from the middle of his torso. My vision kept tunneling, and my body swayed. I couldn't stop the trembling that overtook me as I just kept staring at his paling skin.

"Remiel," Ibis whispered, his voice barely audible. The air filled with the stench of iron as his breath gathered between us. "Don't take me down yet."

"What do you mean?" I muttered back, but I knew he could hear me, this quiet conversation for us and only us.

Always us.

"Everything is—" His body jerked slightly as he shut his eyes tight. He forced a weak smile, his teeth coated in blood. "I don't feel it anymore. I don't want to feel it anymore, Remiel."

"Oh, my sun." A sob snuck past me as I pet back the limp curls hanging damp around Ibis's face. Fresh, hot tears silently fell down my face as I studied him, committing the curve of his jaw and the dimple in his chin to my memory.

"Remiel." Movement caught the corner of my eye, and I noticed Ibis trying to move his hand, the muscles barely twitching. I grabbed his hand in mine, bringing it to cup my cheek, enveloping mine over his.

A smile twitched at the corner of his lips as his face relaxed more. His head leaned heavily into the hand I kept his cheek in. His breathing was shallow, and my mind screamed out at the Gods, at Morana, at Kuk and Khonsa, for taking another thing from me that I loved.

One of the only things I had ever loved so fully, so deeply, with every part of my being.

The familiar darkness pressed in around me the more Ibis's eyes drooped and his breathing slowed. It caressed the recesses of my mind like an old lover, trying to draw me into its embrace.

But I wasn't ready. Not yet.

I wanted to savor every last second gazing upon the sun.

"My soul," Ibis wheezed, forcing himself to meet my eyes. Tears spilled over as the sobs I'd been holding in my chest rushed forward. "Oh, my soul. Find me…"

With one final breath, Ibis's hand and head went slack, the ghost of a smile still left behind as the last person I ever thought I'd lose left me alone in this wretched world.

Chapter 16

Summertide 1799 A.V.

Nearly 10 Years Later

I adjusted the bag on my back, my gaze flickering between the note I'd received via bird carrier and the sign swaying on the old wooden building.

The Red Raven.

I tilted my head to the side as I folded the piece of parchment into a tiny square, shoving it into my pocket. The wooden sign looked worse for wear, but the red paint seemed fresh. It depicted the silhouette of a bird shooting into the sky with its wings spread wide on either side of it.

I swallowed the sharp lump in my throat, reading the words on the sign out loud, "Sing with The Red Raven."

Whoever owned this place even had the audacity to keep the six-pointed Sirian star directly above the beak of the bird.

"Let's get this over with," I grumbled, turning the handle and shoving the door open.

While it wasn't lively by Teslin pub standards, there were a few patrons gathered around a table in front of a fireplace, a man sitting alone in a booth with a stack of papers, and a familiar woman polishing a glass.

At my entrance, every single patron turned their heads toward me, bodies stiffening momentarily.

Until all the Magics in the room realized I was only another Magic who just walked into their pub.

"So, you got our letter," Dahlia chirped from behind the bar, slamming the glass on the bartop with a sly grin. Her brick-red eyes twinkled as they bounced from me to the table of men.

I followed her gaze to where Willem was reclined in one of the chairs, legs spread wide with a cigar hanging from his mouth.

His dull and oily, ash-blond hair hung haphazardly around his head, and wild, untamed stubble spattered his jaw and upper lip. I could even see ink markings peeking out from underneath his tunic, and I shivered at what he did to get those to stick past our enhanced healing.

I pulled the parchment out of my pocket, waving it in the air. "A fucking raven, Dahlia? I'm going to credit every part of whatever this is to you because I know for a fact Willem doesn't give a damn."

All I got from Willem was a grunt of agreement as he tipped the cigar in my direction, paying more attention to whatever game they were playing at his table.

"That was the exact response I got from Willem when I asked him if we should try to find you." Dahlia smirked, folding her hands across her chest. "Now, are you going to have a beer or not?"

I huffed, balling up the parchment and throwing it towards the table. It bounced perfectly in front of Willem, and the corner of his lip twitched before he tossed it into the fire beside him.

I slid onto the barstool, letting my bag fall beside me on the scraped floor. Dahlia placed the beer mug in front of me, some of the golden liquid sloshing over the sides. I nodded once before gulping it back greedily.

"Gods, Remy," Dahlia gawked, snorting. "Parched?"

"I came straight from the port." I slammed the heavy glass down between us, now half-empty. "Took me a minute to get here."

"Why didn't you fly?" Dahlia scowled, her eyes scanning my shoulders.

"I don't fly anymore," I snapped, clenching my fists in my lap and narrowing my eyes at her. "Why did you call me here, Dahlia?"

"I haven't seen you in a decade, not since…" She trailed off, hovering a hand palm-up between us. "I figured it would be good for you to see some familiar faces and surround yourself with friends."

"Let me get this straight." I couldn't help the hysterical chuckle that tumbled from my lips. "You requested my presence—and I need to emphasize again *by raven*—in Eldamain because you wanted to have some grand reunion?"

She shrugged, gnawing at the inside of her lip. Her almond eyes shone with pity as she said, "You know it's not healthy for our kind to be alone for long periods of time, especially after what happened in Lolis. You've been missing this whole time—"

"I can assure you I was not *missing*." I downed the rest of the beer, tapping the rim. She pursed her lips as she snatched the mug and refilled it from the keg. "Truth be told, Dahlia, I have no interest in keeping any more relationships, let alone forming new ones. I don't mind coming to say hello, but I'm not going to stay."

"Oh, and where are you going to go?" She perched her hands on her hips as she slung her towel over her shoulder. "To the Northern Pizi? Whoring it through Teslin? Maybe even venture to Mariande for the holidays?"

"Why wouldn't I do any of that?" I twirled the corners of my mustache, resting my elbow on the bartop. "I have nothing else to do with my life, so as might as well experience all the world has to offer for however long I'm *graced* to live on this fucking plane by the Gods."

"Gods, you're worse than Willem." She shook her head, her eyes flitting across my face, searching for something.

I jerked my thumb over my shoulder toward the table of men. "Him? I find that insulting, Dahl-face. I look immaculate compared to that hobo. Besides, by the looks of him, he's just been existing in life since he lost them. I, on the other hand, have been *living*."

She slammed her hands in front of me, noses nearly touching as she growled, "You've been *running*."

I clenched my teeth, grinding them as my pulse skyrocketed. I averted the intensity of her gaze, staring at a dark brown stain underneath the stool beside me.

I inhaled long and sharp through my nose. "What do you want, Dahlia?"

She pushed herself away to lean back against the counter below the liquor wall. She crossed one leg in front of the other, her jaw set.

"I want you to know I did want to see you," she quietly admits, staring back at the table with Willem. "These ten years have been long, yet simultaneously the shortest decade of my life. The three of us are all that remain from that tragic day. We all lost someone, Remy. We understand your pain more than anyone in the world could ever."

"He wasn't the first person I ever lost to the cruelty of mortals," I whispered, foreign tears prickling the corners of my eyes. I cleared my throat, shaking my head, but unable to say any more.

Losing my parents and Cara had been a living nightmare.

But I'd been in hell every day since Ibis was taken from me.

"It's not all mortals, friend." Dahlia sighed, rubbing her arm. "You have to remember that."

I let out an unintelligible sound, something between a chuckle and a grunt.

"There is another motive behind bringing you here, though. If I recall correctly, you know a thing or two about the Black Avalanches."

I stopped the beer mug mid-journey to my lips, resting the rim on the bottom one. I pressed my eyebrows together, tilting my head to the side as I lowered the mug back down.

"That's a very strange statement." Her face gave away nothing, so I nodded. "It's where I apprenticed with Voss and..." I trailed off, unable to say his name out loud.

She dipped her head in understanding, and her gaze flickered briefly over my shoulder before she continued, "There have been rumors around Main Town that something lives within the mountains. Now, they're just rumors, and some of us don't know the mountains enough to know if anything does live in them, but Karasi assumed you may be able to—"

"Karasi," I deadpanned, lifting an eyebrow. "As in the Great Karasi?"

"The one and only." The corner of her lip quirked up into a smirk. "Anyone who knows the mountains has never lived within them like you did, so we figured you'd be able to tell us if it was some sort of animal, person, or... I don't know."

"Are you guys sure it isn't Voss?" I picked up the glass again. "He's got wings, too, you know."

Something dark passed over Dahlia's face, but it was gone in a blink. I shook my head before letting the liquid pour into my mouth.

"Fine," I agreed in between two large gulps. "I'll go take a look at them. You got a horse I can borrow, though? I'm not walking all the way there. I've done enough walking over the last decade."

"Why don't you use your wings?" She leveled me with a raised eyebrow, taking the empty glass. "I'm sure that's even faster than a horse."

"I. Don't. Fly. Any. More." I stood from the stool, throwing my bag over my shoulder. "You remember the state I found him in when he died?"

Her throat bobbing as she swallowed was confirmation enough for me.

I threw up two fingers over my shoulder as I stalked towards the door. "I'll take up a room at the nearest inn. I hope there's a horse there for me in the morning."

"Hey, Remy," Dahlia called out just as I wrapped my hand around the handle. I peered over my shoulder, eyebrow raised and lips pursed. "In the old days, they believed when a raven crossed your path, it was an omen of change. That everything would be fine."

I let out a single breath of laughter, throwing my middle finger up as I yelled out, "Fuck off, Dahlia."

·⋆⋆⋆☽⋆⋆⋆·

I stood in front of the towering peaks of the Black Avalanches, my heart in my throat.

I was on the complete opposite end of the mountain range on its north-facing side. If I had been blindfolded on my journey over here, I would've told you I was on the side I grew up staring at. I couldn't tell north from south, east from west. Every peak looked just as ominous and menacing as the next.

Looking up, every plateau reminded me of my time spent in the mountains with Voss and Ibis. Both of their voices tickled in the back of my mind, distant memories that still managed to pull the ghost of a smile to my lips.

Flying through the peaks, weaving in and out with flashes of white, the sun glistening off bronzed skin, illuminating whiskey eyes.

Don't you remember, Remiel? It's not polite to stare.

I slammed his voice out of my head, rubbing my chest where I felt a visceral sting beside my heart.

As I approached the base of the mountains, I cursed Dahlia in my mind because nothing looked different about them. Granted, I didn't know what she wanted me to look for other than a sign that something or someone was living in them.

I carefully stepped up a somewhat carved path, the gravel tumbling down the angled slope behind me. I climbed to the nearest plateau before I stopped and glanced down.

I'd maybe climbed a couple hundred feet up the mountains, and considering the amount of hiking and walking I'd become accustomed to in arguably harsher terrain, my chest felt as though someone sat directly on me. It took quite a bit of effort to expand my lungs, but I wasn't fatigued.

I peered around some of the sharper inclines, trying to spot some sort of cave or sign of residence—animal or person. A strange tingling prickled from my lower back and up my spine, and I rolled my shoulders to try and shake the odd sensation.

"What the fuck," I whispered, twisting left and right. I even extended my gaze skyward, searching for signs of a nearby fire.

I had never felt anything within the Black Avalanches, but the feeling assaulting me caused my heart to flutter uncomfortably. I would have attributed it to some sort of traumatic response or anxiety, but I dealt with plenty of those episodes throughout my life, and this was neither.

This was deeper, chilling my bones, every muscle in my body

screaming at me to leave.

As I went to do just that, something around the corner caught my eye. At the same time, a heavy, unpleasant odor surrounded me. The aroma was sharp and bitter, with a hint of smokiness and a faint metallic undertone that reminded me staunchly of blood.

When I turned toward the movement in my peripheral, I froze as every enhanced sense narrowed in on the strange phenomena in front of me.

An unnatural cloud floated in the air, but thick like ink. It was black, too, like the darkest depths of the night sky, but it slithered through the air like blood in water. The smell continued to invade me, and my ears faintly rang, so sharp and high-pitched that it grated at my skin.

I screamed out in pain and shock as my wings sprung unjustifiably from my back for the first time in ten years.

I fell to my knees, hissing as the rocks bit into my skin. I clenched my fists, my nails biting, the sting spearing through the muscles in my back.

"Godsdamnit," I growled through my teeth. My chest heaved in winds of breath, and I gradually lifted my head to where the dark mass had been.

But I was alone once again.

"Fascinating," a scratchy yet feminine voice broke through my haze. I spun in my hunch to face the stranger before me.

The foreign woman towered over me despite the fact she would be over a foot shorter than me if I stood at my full height. Her dark ebony skin glistened in the shining sun, and dark chocolate dreads hung down her curvaceous body. There were some wrinkles around her eyes, mouth, and forehead, maybe placing her in her early middle ages.

But I knew that was a deceiving thought because her beady

yellow eyes studied me, the vertical slits for pupils all-knowing.

"I have known very few from the House of Echidna to be marked by the Gods," the Magic before me declared. "And yet, here you are, baring the wings of a *drakon*."

"You know the old Etherean language," I sighed, still trying to catch my breath. I uncurled from my crouch, standing over her. "And you know the animal we reign from."

"We?" She tilted her head imperceptibly, but her face gave away nothing. "And you suppose I hail from Echidna?"

I waved my hand listlessly between us. "The eyes. Reptilian, no?"

The smallest smirk twitched at the corner of her lips, and those eerie eyes twinkled. "You have been educated in the Houses quite thoroughly, I suppose."

"You suppose?" I rolled my shoulders, snapping my wings back into my body. I stumbled forward, and she raised an eyebrow.

"You are Remiel, are you not?" She beckoned me to follow her out of the mountain range from the way I came.

How the *fuck* did I not hear her?

"It's Remy, thanks." I tried to watch where I walked while keeping an eye on her. She barely lowered her head to her feet, staring in front of her as though she knew the path well. "You're the Great Karasi, aren't you?"

"It's Karasi," she corrected, throwing her head over her shoulder, "thanks."

I scoffed, unable to hide the smile from my face. But it fell as I remembered what I just encountered in the mountains. "The Black Avalanches... What's going on with them?"

She stopped abruptly, taking one last look over her shoulder.

"I take it you brought a horse?" After I nodded, she continued, "We shall ride back to my home together. Some things are better discussed in private, away from prying ears and eyes."

We made it back to her shack of a home, smaller than what Ibis and I owned in Lolis. It had two bedrooms, a living area, and a kitchen, but the latter were practically the same room.

Gods, the ridiculous man cave of Voss's was larger than this place.

"I don't spend much time in this home." Karasi waved a wrinkled hand littered with jewelry. "I travel quite often, and it is just myself who lives here."

"So I've heard," I grumbled, waiting for her to take a seat at her kitchen table before following suit. "You asked Dahlia to summon me. Why not summon Voss? The old man has lived in those mountains for Gods-know how long."

"Voss died four years ago, Remy," Karasi announced nonchalantly. "I apologize that I'm the one to break this news to you."

I thought I'd be sad to hear he passed, but all I felt was a strange twinge in my sternum. I rubbed it, frowning. "How did he die? Was it age?"

"Long ago, the Gods decided that our world required balance," Karasi randomly blurted, staring into me. "Another being fated with a great power emerged, another of equal caliber had to leave this world."

A strange shiver ran up my arms, leaving gooseflesh in its path. I visibly shook it off and leaned back into the chair, putting some distance between us. "Well, if that isn't ominous. Do you always talk like this? In jilted, vague sentences."

"Some have found it a nuisance." Karasi folded her hands on the table. "Another version of myself would have probably found it a nuisance many, many years ago. But alas, that is how the clock goes round. You know a thing or two about being different people, do you not?"

I wanted to call her crazy, to walk out the door and never look back, but I felt nailed to the chair beneath me. The way she spoke was captivating in an entirely different way than Voss spoke, and I found myself knowing exactly what she meant.

Magics had always lived extended lifetimes. Voss didn't look older than his mid-thirties when he was my mentor. At the ripe age of thirty-five, I still looked like I was in my early or mid-twenties.

Life was ever changing for us, the world moving at the same pace despite our existence.

Before Ibis, I was wild and reckless. During our co-apprenticeship, I was flighty but ambitious. Being with Ibis, I never felt more joy and peace. After him, I was a soulless vagabond.

What was next for me?

"So, what's going on with the mountains?" I asked again, interlocking my arms over the table.

"Did your mentor ever tell you about the Abyss?" Karasi asked, gauging my reaction.

"He didn't need to," I admitted quietly, barely above a whisper.

The Abyss was what Magic parents used to threaten you with to get you to behave. It was an ancient evil that lurked beneath the Black Avalanches, waiting to rise again. My parents used to tell Cara and me that if we acted out, the Abyss would come out from the mountains to claim little Magic's lives.

As I got older I understood the version told to children was a little dramatic, but it was still a myth and threat the Magic community always revered.

It was prophesied that a strange, foreign Abyss would inhabit the mountains, hinting at Kuk's return.

That only meant something to those who believed in the Gods.

I met Karasi's penetrating gaze only to find a milky white muting the vibrant yellow of her eyes. I startled in my seat as she spoke, "If the Abyss lives, Darkness has risen again."

I blinked, and her eyes returned to their natural state. She sat there as if nothing happened. "What's that supposed to mean?"

"Long ago, the Abyss would rise when the power of the Dark Sirians would," she spoke confidently. "It has returned, which means Sirians are wielding the Dark power in our world."

"The Sirians can't actually be completely gone." I rubbed the side of my arm. "How do they develop Light or Dark?"

"If they grow to fear themselves and the power they wield, they will bring forth the Darkness," she explained, reaching for a black stone in the middle of the table.

It uncannily resembled Ibis's pendant.

"Wouldn't every Sirian child that's been shunned since the Korbins nearly wiped them out wield Darkness, then?" I asked, watching her fiddle with it in her hands. "The whole world fears them."

"Not always," she shrugged, letting the hematite tumble back to the table with a scowl. "But now there are enough of them, or one powerful enough, to summon the Abyss back."

I considered what she said about Voss, so I tilted my head, the cogs turning in my head. "It was a Sirian, wasn't it? Who Voss had to die?"

She didn't look at me, just fixated her gaze on the table. "The Sirian should be in their early childhood. Their power should form within the next decade, and for now, this child's fate will lead them into the Darkness. But by the Abyss in the mountains, I would say others are wielding the Darkness already."

I sat back in my seat with a heavy sigh, and stared over her shoulder across her hut, contemplating.

Like wondering what the *fuck* I was doing here.

"Well, this has been an interesting history lesson," I grunted as I lifted myself from the chair, using my hands on the table as a boost, "and it was great meeting you. But Dahlia summoned me to figure out what was going on, and based on this entire conversation, you only needed me to confirm a suspicion you already had.

"So, I will take my leave and be on my merry way." I started to move toward the door, but her voice broke through the house like an arrow straight to my heart.

"You run from the memory of him." Tears sprung up, burning like the fires that raged around me the night he died. A single tear fell as I stood frozen in the middle of the room. "What would your *soul* say if he knew that you refuse to think of him in life?"

"No." I pivoted on my heel, leveling a finger at her. "You do not get to speak of him. You did not know him. No one knew him as I knew him. He was my heart, and he took it with him when he left me."

"The dead never leave us willingly," she stated, as simple as the weather. "It is okay to believe that a part of you went with him when he died. But a part of him also *stayed* with you."

The tears silently ran down my cheeks, his beautiful eyes flashing in my mind. I clenched my jaw against the ache in my bones, in my soul, from where he had been ripped from me.

"Do not forget what existed between the beginning and the end," she said with finality, rising from her seat. "For while he may be gone, you have much to live yet before you are reunited with your other half. You will do well to spend your time doing anything other than running."

"So, what do I do until then?" My lip trembled as my vision wavered. "Where do I go? I have no one. I have nothing."

"There is a place for those who have lost and do not know who they are anymore, who do not know where to go." Karasi swept her hand toward the direction of the Black Avalanches but, more importantly, toward the direction of Main Town.

The Forgotten City of Eldamain.

Chapter 17

Midwinter 1806 A.V.

Over 6 Years Later

I sat at the regular table beside Willem, dealing out the cards between him and me, twin cigars dangling from our lips. Just as the last card landed on top of his pile, the front door of The Red Raven burst open, a cold winter draft rushing in with the intruder.

"What the hell, Dahlia?" Willem grumbled, curling a lip at her as he hugged his flannel tighter, shivering. "You're gonna let all the heat out."

"Bite me," she hissed, dropping into the seat in front of me. After knocking back her hood, she folded her arms over the table. "When was the last time any of you heard from Karasi?"

I frowned up at her, setting my cigar in the ashtray and shrugging.

Willem tapped the burnt shavings of his cigar into the tray. "Time is just an illusion we use to measure our slow march toward inevitable disappointment and decay."

I chuckled under my breath, shaking my head. "Would you shut the fuck up?"

Dahlia snapped out a single claw from her nailbed, jabbing Willem in the shoulder with a soft *thunk*, snarling. "I'm not talking to you. Remy's the better of us at tracking time."

"I couldn't tell you," I said, but my mind already started working on the math.

This was the seventeenth winter without Ibis, which meant I showed up in Eldamain seven years ago. The last time I'd seen Karasi was when I delivered her quite a hefty supply of dried artemisia, comfrey, and vervain leaf about…

"Holy shit," I whispered, staring at a deep gauge in the wooden tabletop. I cleared my throat, meeting Dahlia's brick-red gaze. "I haven't talked to her in five years."

Dahlia's head drooped, and she gawked at me with her mouth open. Willem stopped shuffling the cards to look up at us through his lashes.

"What's the big deal?" he mumbled around his cigar, waving a hand in the air. "She goes on random adventures all the time. Five years is nothing to us."

"Okay," Dahlia drawled, scoffing. "But it's a long time when there are rumors in town that *no one* has seen or heard anything from her. Not even a letter."

"Are you two screwing?" Willem narrowed his eyes, slipping his cigar onto one of the grooves of the tray. "A little old for you—"

"Would you shut *up?*" Dahlia growled, her claws snapping out.

I placed a hand between the two of them on the table. "Alright, dumb and dumber." I leveled Willem with another warning glare before directing my attention to Dahlia. "When has Karasi ever given the impression that she should report her whereabouts to anyone? Just because she's drawn the three of us into Eldamain doesn't mean she's our… mother."

Dahlia leaned back in her chair, frowning. "I guess you're right. I don't know… I just have a weird feeling. She was so concerned about those stupid mountains, I didn't think she'd want them out of her sight."

"They aren't," a deep voice rumbled from a nearby booth. Dahlia and I lifted our heads to the corner closest to the bar to find Rol, the owner of The Red Raven, his eyes flitting over some parchment.

"What do you mean?" Dahlia gawked, angling her body toward him.

He quickly marked something with a quill before slowly glancing our way. "The mountains haven't left her sight. Someone was here the other day asking for her and one of the locals said she's there but not taking visitors."

"And you didn't think to tell us she's been home this whole time?" Dahlia's eyes were as wide as the coasters on the table. I rolled mine as Rol chuckled to himself, reverting his attention back to his things.

"Dahlia," Willem laughed—actually *laughed*. I curled a lip at him, leaning away. "This is the first time I've even heard you ask where Karasi is. Don't act like you haven't been lost in whatever you've been up to these days to go check on her."

"I mean, I know better than to show up on Karasi's doorstep uninvited." Dahlia ran a hand through her cropped hair. "It's just odd she hasn't left the house. How has she been eating or getting supplies?"

"I will say I delivered a ton of supplies to her the last time I saw her." I shrugged, taking a quick swig of my beer. "Maybe she stocked up and is on a spiritual journey that we shouldn't disrupt."

"If her spiritual journey includes a child," Rol muttered under his breath, but all three of us heard him loud and clear as we snapped our heads to Rol with various forms of shock slapped onto our faces.

"Excuse me?" I sputtered, leaning forward on the table. "What do you mean a *child*?"

Rol shrugged, not bothering to look up from whatever he was doing in his booth today. "There've been a few rumors of a small child running amuck on her land. Don't know how old or much else, just that a small human has been inhabiting, too."

"A small human," I said at the same time Dahlia grumbled, "What in the Gods is going on?"

We connected gazes across the table, and the minute she raised an eyebrow at me, I knew what she was asking.

"Why do I have to go?" I groaned, tugging at my hair. "You lot have known her longer."

"You have wings, so you'll get there faster." Dahlia unfurled her hand between us. "Besides, I think she likes you better anyway."

I exhaled a breath just as slowly as I inhaled, flaring my nostrils.

I had used my wings two other times in the past seven years since the Abyss in the mountains forced them out. Both had been at Karasi's request, who simply asked because she wanted to see them. Dahlia knew I hadn't used them nearly as frequently as she was accustomed to, and she also knew it wasn't hard for Karasi to coax them out of me.

"That or you're walking," Dahlia smirked in a challenge. "Either way, you're checking in on her."

⋆˚🌙˚⋆

Landing in the fresh snow stretching across Karasi's plot, I curled my wings back painfully. The lack of use in almost two decades had taken its toll on my ability to freely call them to me.

Not to mention the images I'd battled the entire flight over of brighter, feathery wings coated in sticky blood.

Something rose from the ground directly in front of me,

its small head searching but not quite seeing me, which wasn't surprising given the sun's glare.

Taking in its size, I realized quickly the rumors Rol claimed were true.

Karasi had a child.

"What in the Gods?" I yelped, startling it. Said child jumped from its seated position, standing frozen in the snow with its arms stiff at its sides.

Not it... *Her.*

The young girl's hair fell around her shoulders in long, matted curls that reminded me of Cara, except the color was black like a raven's feather. Even from this distance, I could tell her olive-toned skin was covered in smudges of dirt, the clothes she wore swallowing her up. She looked petrified, her bright eyes round.

Something about her tugged at me like a fish on a reel.

I carefully put one foot in front of the other, gradually lowering to the ground as I got closer to her. When I was forced to my knees, I crawled to her until I could reach out a hand to caress her arm.

She didn't register my touch, still stunned at the sight of me, her eyes twitching over my face.

Which allowed me to behold the scar in the middle of her forehead.

Not a small mortal child.

A small *Sirian* child.

Fucking Gods, Karasi.

"Who are you, kid?" I asked her, and something snapped her out of her stupor. She stumbled backward into the snow, falling onto a half-finished snowman.

If I really was the last person to see Karasi in the last five years, this child looked to be around that age.

Karasi hadn't socialized this child for five years.

"I won't harm you," I pleaded softly, holding out my hand to her. Her golden eyes, two shades lighter than Ibis's, bounced between my hand and my face, hesitantly assessing. "I'm a friend of Karasi's."

I didn't know how to convince her, so I shot my claws out to try and demonstrate to her I was Magic, someone safe who understood the need for secrecy.

Fat load of good that did because she gasped, a small squeak that broke my heart, sliding further into the snow pile beneath her.

I pressed my lips together, trying to talk around my canines that wouldn't help any if she noticed them. "Is Karasi home?" I sighed, my chest heaving. "Who am I kidding… She's not stupid enough to leave a young kid home by herself."

The child dipped her head, burying her chin into her chest, as she kept her eyes trained on me.

Was she giving me *puppy dog* eyes? I couldn't help the twitch at the corner of my lips. This child had seemingly been raised by the ever-stoic Karasi, but she knew how to really punch you in the heart.

But I didn't know how the hell Karasi got this child. It surely wasn't hers because there wasn't an ounce of resemblance between the two, not to mention the color of her skin was toffee and warm compared to Karasi's cooler ebony tone.

I vocalized as much. "Well, you're not hers, that's for sure. Did she pick you up off the side of the road?"

What I didn't expect was for the child to answer my rhetorical question. "I've been here my whole life."

And that voice sang to me like a melody I forgot I knew. It wrapped around my heart, clenching it in a vice. I had to blink away the tears that prickled uncharacteristically at the corners of my eyes, frowning.

"And how old are you?" I couldn't look away from that damning Mark on her forehead.

If Karasi had her since infancy, what was her plan?

The kid sat up a little straighter, crisscrossing her legs. Apparently, she enjoyed this question because she nearly slapped all five of her fingers in my face and yelped, "I'm five!"

"Five," I whispered under my breath. Gods, Karasi really was here with a child this entire time. "Will you give me your name, kid?"

"I'm—"

"What in the Gods' names are you doing here?" Karasi shouted from the porch.

The child and I both launched to our feet, and she clung to my pant leg, digging her little hands into the fabric. I stared down at the top of her head, raising my arms. I followed her line of sight to where Karasi stood menacingly, her fists clenched at her sides.

"What am I doing here?" I couldn't help the hysterical chuckle that fell from my lips. I leaned my body slightly away from the child still stuck to my leg, angling both of my hands toward the top of her head. "What the fuck is this, Karasi?"

She continued to glare at me, rage like I'd never seen radiating across the lawn, those piercing yellow eyes assessing me.

"You're gone for *five years*, and you expect all of us not to come looking for you?" I shouted, nearly taking a step forward before remembering there was a *Sirian girl* glued to me.

Glancing down, I found her already staring up at me, those eyes glistening. I raised an eyebrow, but she gave me those fucking doe eyes again. I bent down, slipping my hands under her armpits.

I hauled her against me, and she instantly wrapped her small arms around my neck, ripping a subtle gasp from my lungs. I collected myself and made my way towards the hut with the girl in my arms.

"I'm honored it took you all so long to check up on me." Karasi crossed her arms over her chest, shifting her weight to one leg. While she tried to exude her nonchalance, I noticed the stiffness in her shoulders.

"You're prone to travels, and we all have our own shit to deal with." I winced, realizing I needed to watch my mouth around this kid. "In fact, I thought you'd be dead before I ever saw you with a child."

"Karasi is dying?" The child yanked her head off my shoulder, staring at me wide-eyed.

I pressed my lips together before glaring at the kid. "No, nobody is dying—"

"I wouldn't count on that yet," Karasi interrupted, leveling me with a scowl.

"You think I'm going to tell people about the kid?" I scoffed, shaking my head. The girl looked between Karasi and me with her small hands resting on my chest, observing. "Do I seem like someone who is going to turn you and a child over because of what she is?"

"The less people that know about her, the better." Karasi twisted on her heel, storming into her hut.

I sighed, following after her and ducking under the threshold. "You can't possibly think you can handle her on your own. You have entrusted me, Dahlia, and Willem with quite a lot over the years, and you didn't consider trusting us with this? For fucks sake, Willem actually knows what it's like to raise kids, especially girls—"

"Formerly a father or not, I wouldn't trust the cynic with a child," Karasi snapped, throwing her arm toward the girl. "Besides, none of you know how to raise a Sirian child. This is my burden to carry."

"Do you think it's healthy to hide a child away from existence?" I tried to peel said child away from me, but she locked her arms tighter around my neck. I glared at Karasi as I lowered myself to one of the chairs at her kitchen table. "First of all, she is clinging to a stranger. She is desperate for contact, Karasi. Second of all, why is she so damn filthy? Are you bathing her?"

Karasi just stared at me from the other side of her small hut, lips pursed. I adjusted the kid on my lap so she faced the center of the table. I watched in horror as she reached for an open vial of what looked like hemlock resting in the middle of the table.

I moved faster than she could register, throwing the vial toward the sink. "How 'bout we don't play with the poison, huh?"

She frowned at me with a pout, lowering her head like I'd scolded her.

I turned my attention back to Karasi. "What did you plan on doing once her Light manifests? I get you have prophetic gifts and some other things, but you don't have any Magic abilities that manifest into a physical element. I'm the only one amongst our crew with an animate gift. If anything, you should've told *me* about her. I'll have to be the one to teach her control one day."

"I have helped hundreds of Sirians in my lifetime." She finally joined us at the table, sliding a literal stick over to the girl. For the love of the Gods… "I have the means necessary to access any educational material she will need."

"Okay, but you'll have to teach her how to read first." The girl grabbed some stray fabric and began tying it around various points of the stick. "I have a feeling you haven't taught her that yet."

"Oh, Gods, Remy." Karasi slumped into her chair, rubbing her temple. "I'm not completely incapable of raising a child."

"Well, at least you've been doing that," I grumbled, rubbing my thumb across a speckle of dirt on her cheek. "Daily baths must be where your knowledge—"

"Do not come to my home uninvited and patronize me, boy." Karasi pointed a knobby finger at me, resting her elbow on the table. "You don't know the first thing about this child. She loves playing outside from the moment the sun rises over the horizon until it sets again. She is fed, monitored, bathed, lo—" Karasi stopped herself, lowering her hand as her gaze snagged onto the child.

"Loved?" I finished for her, unintentionally tightening my grip on the kid. "Is she, Karasi? Are you capable of that?"

Actual tears lined Karasi's eyes briefly, but she blinked them away and averted her gaze. I looked back down at the girl, who was already watching me with sheer, unadulterated curiosity.

A small grin graced her face, lighting up her eyes. She extended her hand to me, offering the stick she'd been decorating with ribbons.

"I made it for you," she squeaked softly, urging me to accept it. "I make them for Karasi every day, so you can have this one since you're here now, too."

My chest tightened as I happily accepted the gift from her, twirling it between my finger and thumb. I glanced back up at Karasi, and I followed her gaze to where she was looking toward the wall above her couch.

Sure enough, sticks of various sizes covered every inch of the wall, with different-colored ribbons tied around them.

I turned my head back to Karasi. She regarded the child in my arms, who had decided to recline against my chest. I couldn't help the hand that pet down her wild hair, pinching the end of a strand between my fingers.

"What are you to her?" I asked Karasi quietly.

"Her guardian." Karasi shrugged, meeting my gaze. "Her mentor."

I twisted the strand around my finger, marveling at how small she felt in my arms. I wanted to draw her in closer, keep her safe, watch over her like I should've watched over all the things I'd loved in my life.

"And what do you suppose you'll be to her?" Karasi folded her hands on the table. "*If* you were to be part of her life."

Anything. I didn't know where that answer came from, but the child in my arms somehow managed to work her way under my skin, striking a sensitive nerve.

Maybe it was the way she reminded me of Cara, the wild hair and spirit I could see dancing in her eyes.

Maybe it was those eyes, the way they were barely two shades lighter than those that stared back when I closed mine.

All I knew was I would be whatever she wanted me to be. A friend, a protector, a guardian, a brother, a father…

I would go to the ends of this world to ensure she always knew what it meant to be loved.

I cleared my throat, willing away the burning in my chest. I tapped the top of her head with the stick, bouncing my leg once to get her attention. She turned sleepy eyes on me, the ghost of that serene grin still lingering at the corners of her lips.

"I didn't get your name, kid." I poked her in the side, eliciting the most angelic giggle I'd ever heard. "Who are you, stranger?"

"Reva." She smiled wide before burrowing into my arms, just as she would burrow deep into the rest of my life.

From that moment on, whatever pieces of my soul hadn't died with Ibis now belonged to Reva, my glowing star in the darkest nights.

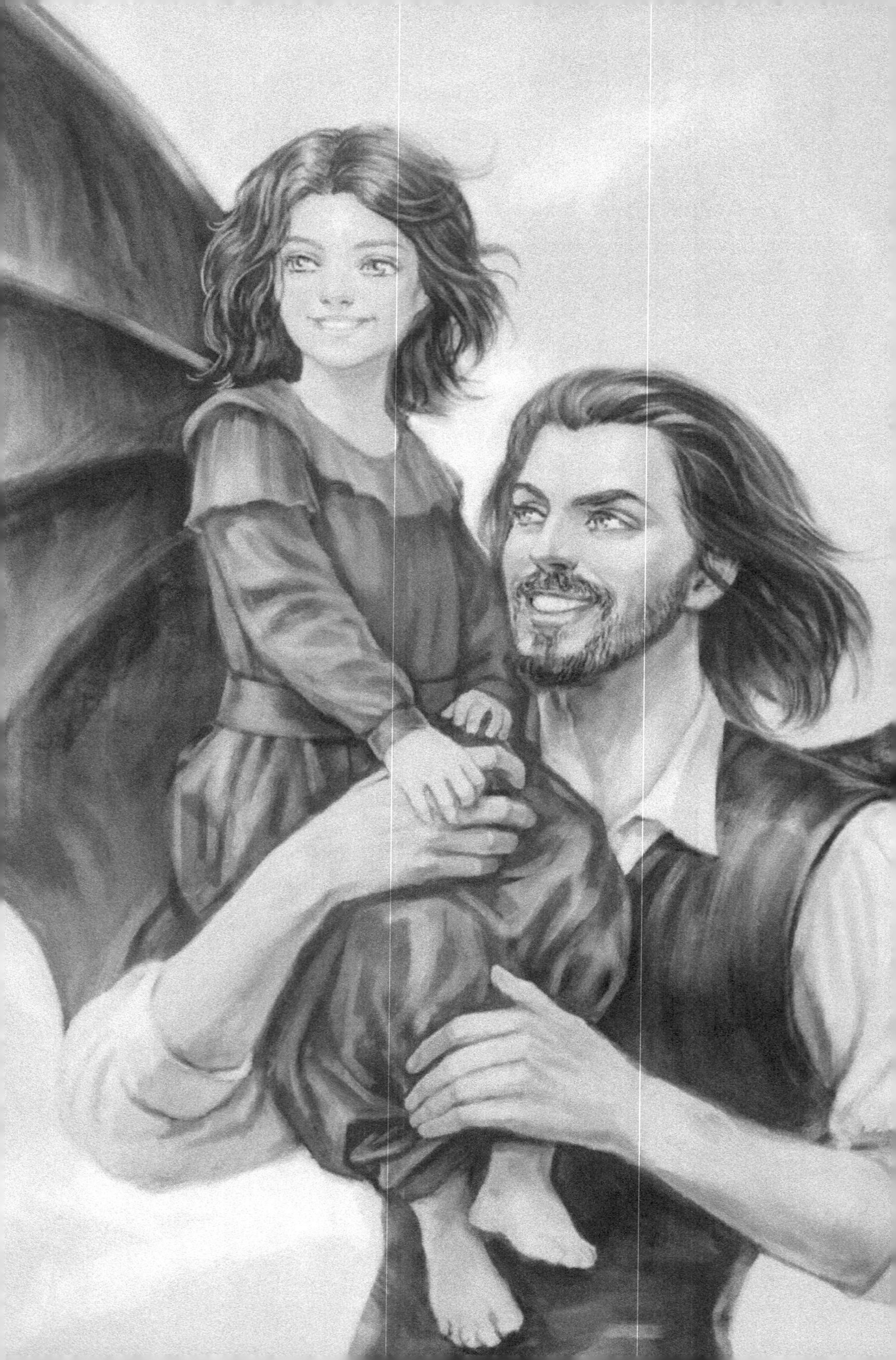

Epilogue
Springtide 1823 A.V.

Over 17 Years Later

She sat on the ground beside the Crown Prince of Mariande, conversing enthusiastically about something with Willem and Dahlia, who were not nearly as enthused as she or the prince. The longer the conversation went on, the more frustrated both Reva and Willem became while the prince just held himself quite patiently. Even Dahlia grew more irritated the longer he talked, but I could see her gaze from across the lawn bouncing between Reva and Prince Tariq.

He mumbled something to the small group before turning and walking across the lawn towards me, the princess, and the knight who accompanied them on this trip for Reva.

So Reva could help us bury the Great Karasi.

I raised an eyebrow as he approached, but he just offered a tightlipped grin as he gestured towards his sister, Princess Eloise, and offered his assistance in sorting their supplies into their tents.

When I looked back at Reva, the look on her face as she watched Prince Tariq walk away was not lost on me.

Like he was the sun that brought light into her world.

Gods, was I familiar with that look, and my heart both ached and soared for her.

It didn't take long after Dahlia's giggle traveled on the wind for Reva to lurch from her seat, shouting to her and Willem that they were acting like children.

"You seem to be replacing people just fine," I heard Dahlia say, and I winced as I folded a blanket and passed it to the knight, Finley.

"She laying into them?" he asked, those beautiful green eyes catching in the sun.

I shook my head, marveling at how handsome he was. Gods, what was in Mariande's water? "More like they're laying into her. Seems they're jealous of the relationships she's built with you lot."

Finley frowned at Reva, where she bit back at Dahlia about how her life was not some glamorous dream, waving her hands around like she was swatting flies away. "She mentioned they like to give her a hard time."

I shrugged, turning to allow the trio some privacy. "Their connection to Reva is difficult. They've both lost people they've cared about, so it's difficult for them to express that."

"And you?" Finley followed to where I grabbed a crate with ease before shoving it into his arms. "She talks more about you than the others, so it seems like the relationship the two of you have may have been healthier. Have you lost anyone?"

My heart swelled at his comment on her talking about me more, but I just shrugged with my hands up. "Of course I have. I just handled it differently than they did. Besides, between you and me, that girl's had me in her clutches since the moment I met her."

We both watched as Reva *marched* to her tent, throwing back the flap before disappearing inside, presumably using her firepower to flick the lamp to life within.

I clapped my hand over the poor kid's shoulder as his gaze lingered on her tent, leaning down to his ear. "I have a feeling you know what I'm talking about."

I gave his shoulder a nice one-two pat before making my way to Reva's tent.

After pulling back the flap enough to peek my head in, I cleared my throat to announce myself. Sitting on the cot with her elbows on her thighs and her head in her hands, she sneered up at me from between her fingers.

I couldn't help the chuckle that slipped from my lips as I stepped in, allowing the flap to sway behind me. I waved my hand over the cot. "May I?"

She nodded as she rubbed her hands down her face.

I quietly sat beside her, slinging an arm over her shoulder. She leaned into my chest.

"How are you doing, kid?" I asked, which elicited a breathy chuckle from her. I shook my head, rubbing my hand against her arm. "I know it's been a lot, but I think you're doing pretty damn well."

"I'd be inclined to disagree," she sighed, lifting her head to look up at me. Her voice softened, cracking slightly as she said, "It feels like I'm tearing in half."

My heart broke at how fragile she appeared then, especially when all I could see was that small child that clung to my pant leg the day I met her.

"Aren't we all," I mumbled, turning my head away from her. I could relate to that feeling more than she knew, which also reminded me of the Crown Prince and what I heard Dahlia say on the winds. "I have to admit, Dahlia did catch onto something I noticed when I flew into Mariande. Her approach was a little half-ass backward, but what do you expect from her?"

"If you're talking about Tariq," Reva said quietly, almost in warning. "Then this discussion ends here."

The smile that broke across my face felt so foreign as I was reminded of another who once fought love every step of the way. "You would make a fine match. The way you two are already in tune with one another—"

"Remy." She groaned as she uncurled from underneath my arm, glaring at me with the exhaustion of someone far older than twenty-two. "There are way too many variables for me to digest where I stand emotionally with Tariq. I could think of a number of reasons why it would not work out. I don't have time—"

"For happiness?" My face dropped as I glimpsed the same hopelessness I felt when I'd secluded myself in Teslin. "I know you think you may have to carry the world on your shoulders, but for the love of the Gods, Reva, do not forget to find happiness in it all. Let yourself have love, no matter how short of a time it might last. Otherwise, you'll look back one day and regret all the moments you spent resisting it when you could have been relishing it."

If I closed my eyes, it was almost like Ibis was beside me at that moment. His warmth—a warmth that I thought long gone—wrapped around me and spread through me as every happy memory between us flashed through my mind.

From the moment we met until some of our final days together, the laughter and joy and peace…

I would relive every part of our journey just to have him in my arms one more time.

I considered Reva missing out on those beautiful moments because she thought she didn't deserve them or could dedicate time to them. I didn't want that for her. I wanted her to have love and happiness, no matter how short it lasted.

While mine was but a blip in my existence, a half of a decade to my nearly sixty years of life…

Everything about Ibis would be forever a part of me, for any light and love I had to give her was because of him, and the things I learned from him and because of him had led me to Reva.

The third greatest love I'd ever known next to him and my family.

"You deserve happiness and love, Reva. Without it, there is nothing to fight for... Nothing to die for."

"It's strange coming from you," she said, tilting her head to the side. My smile returned as I rubbed my thumb across her cheekbone and silently regretted all the things I should've shared with her instead of keeping them to myself.

Maybe there would still be time for me to tell her what it was like to bask in the rays of a sun.

"I'm old enough to have loved at least once, girl," I sighed, shaking Ibis's whiskey eyes from my mind. "Don't be so shocked that I know what I'm talking about. I may not be Karasi, but I have a few words of wisdom up my sleeve."

She quietly observed me through soft, narrowed eyes, her gaze flickering from mine to my mustache and around me like she was reading me.

Suddenly, a smile cracked her exterior, and she flung herself into my arms, wrapping her own around my neck. I instantly squeezed her against me, exhaling as the familiarity of her embrace sang to my very soul.

"I've never thanked you," she whispered against me, still holding on. "For always being what I needed."

I clung to her as I asked, "And what was that?"

She squeezed once as she answered, "A friend, but more importantly... a father."

I nearly choked on a sob as I held back the tears.

I think fatherhood could suit us both beautifully one day.

I tightened my grip on her and hoped for dear life that I

wouldn't lose my girl in this encroaching war.

IF YOU LOVED THE WORLD OF AVEESH...

Continue the Sirians Series with Reva, the child that managed to wrap Remy around her finger.

IF THE ABYSS LIVES, DARKNESS HAS RISEN AGAIN.

Darkness Comes Again is the first book in The Sirians Series, a planned five-book epic fantasy romance series that follows the ever-reluctant, black-cat FMC Reva as she struggles to discover her heritage and who—and what—she really is. This slow-burn, friends-to-lovers series is perfect for readers who love unique magic systems, romantic tension, witty banter, and want something new in their adult fantasy books. This book is meant for readers who enjoy long game, plot-heavy romantasy.

Acknowledgements

When I first started the Sirians Series, I knew the characters I wanted to write novellas for. Remy was not one of them, but when I finally put him on the page in *Darkness Comes Again*, and he slowly made his way back in again with *Fate Demands Sacrifice*, I realized very quickly that he had a story to tell. Not just because there are a lot of easter eggs in this book that connect to the main books of the Sirians Series, but because his love story and growth spoke to me on so many levels.

If you cried reading this, know that I cried harder writing and editing it. This was the first time I ever cried writing a book that had to do with character deaths, and it tore me apart. It was one of the most challenging things I've ever written in more ways than one, but I feel like I healed a lot of things during this process.

I wanted to use this acknowledgments section to thank a few people specifically. But, as always, I am so grateful to those who have contributed to the publication of this novella.

First, to the writers of the *From Loathing to Lovers Collection:* C.A. Blooming, Lindsey N. Rhoden, Jessa Grey, Joanna McSpadden, and T.M. Mayfield—thank you all for coming with me on this journey to get this collection out there. It has been nothing short of *epic*, and it wouldn't be the same without you all.

Next is to my sensitivity reader, Sandor—you were the first person to reach out to me organically when I published DCA and told me how much you loved the story. Thank you for helping me make this story absolutely amazing and making sure that I didn't represent a group incorrectly. It means the world that you were willing to be that reader for me!

To all of my early readers—thank you for being the test subjects on just how heartbreaking this story is and sending me pictures of you sobbing as you read. I only felt bad for a millisecond before I clenched my fist in a *yes* because that was my goal.

To keep this short and sweet, and last but not least, Jake—thank you for supporting me through every part of this journey and willingly reading my stories. *You are my sun, my moon, and all of my stars.*

About the Author

K.M. "Katie" Davidson is an adult fantasy author. Her authorial journey began as a young writer creating YA fantasy novels in composition notebooks and publishing them on Wattpad. After getting her Bachelor's in Creative Writing and Master's in English Literature—and abandoning 20+ book ideas—she finally sat down in 2023 and finished her debut novel, *Darkness Comes Again,* Book 1 of the Sirians Series.

Outside of writing and reading, Katie is a Content Marketer. She loves dance parties with her husband and dog, hiking, traveling, entertaining conspiracy theories (none more than aliens), collecting more rocks, and buying old copies of books published over 100 years ago.

For exclusive sneak peeks, character aesthetics, and more news, follow K.M. Davidson on social media: @kmdavidsonbooks

www.ingramcontent.com/pod-product-compliance
Ingram Content Group UK Ltd.
Pitfield, Milton Keynes, MK11 3LW, UK
UKHW042324200125
453745UK00012BB/51/J